YO-BSD-197

JACK FINNEY

Good Neighbor Sam

SIMON AND SCHUSTER

NEW YORK • 1963

LIBRARY OF CONGRESS CATALOG CARD NUMBER: 63-15365
MANUFACTURED IN THE UNITED STATES OF AMERICA
BY BOOK PRESS, INC., BRATTLEBORO, VERMONT

FOR MARG

1

*C*ALL me Sam.

I'm not going to say what kind of work I do in the offices of Burke & Hare on Montgomery Street to which I drive each weekday morning. I don't want to hurt anyone's feelings so I'll only say that if I and my fellows ever stopped what we do there each day, something terrible might happen, such as you buying another brand of toothpaste. On Friday nights when I leave, I play that if I can drive across Golden Gate Bridge without being forced to the side by a car—company name on the door panel, siren going, red light flashing—that I have escaped into Marin County which has no extradition treaty with San Francisco, and that I don't ever have to go back to the office.

Tonight I just made it, a company car shooting at my tires, Mr. Burke leaning out the driver's window shaking his fist as my wheels touched the blessed Marin County soil, and now I swung off the main highway and onto the road that winds down through the hills and then along the Bay to the sea-level main street of Sausalito. This is a straight narrow street, and for nearly a mile before you reach the shopping area, it is separated by only a sidewalk from the Bay beside it; across the water San Francisco lies spread out on its hills. But nice as the view was, and I never got tired of it, I hadn't taken the long way home through Sausalito for the view but to stop at the dump just north of town.

It wasn't actually a dump but a narrow peninsula of fill pushed out into the Bay for what would presently become a small-boat landing; no garbage allowed, only earth fill and hard junk such as car bodies. But it still looked and smelled like a dump, and I pulled off the road onto it. It was August, plenty of daylight left, sunny and warm, but I kept my suit coat, tie, and hat on. I always enjoyed the puzzled looks from other commuters driving past and seeing me—dressed as they were and apparently one of them—loading junk into the back of a station wagon. My scavenging took on the purifying quality of an act of rebellion, however small, and if I'd owned a rolled umbrella I'd have brought it along.

Tonight I made a particularly good haul; six battered hub caps, the cogs from a little portable cement mixer, and the axle from a kid's wagon with two wheels attached. The tires were gone, but that suited me because the grooves in which they'd been would take a movable belt.

I drove on, rejoining the main highway for several miles, then turned off it onto a paralleling service road, and then off that onto the street I live on. Marin County is all valleys and hills, one of them actually being a small mountain—Tamalpais—visible from all over the county. My street winds between two rows of hills along a little valley that was once a creek bed. There is only a single row of houses on each side of the street, none up on the hills, though I expect to wake up any morning and find the hills bulldozed level and replaced with apartments. But it hasn't happened yet, and it's a nice place to live, the street lined with big evergreens along the curbs.

Driving along it now past the shingle-roofed houses, kids' bikes, parked cars, and people watering lawns, waving at those I knew, it seemed to me that, statistically speaking, this street ought to be about ready to produce a good murder, rape, aggravated assault, or at least a divorce, attempted arson, or a fine case of adultery. These are just a few of the fascinating shenanigans that go on all the time in the tract-housing developments I read about in books from the drugstore, and by any reasonable test Treasure Island is a tract. Instead of a downtown with a main street, we have an enormous shake-shingled shopping center in the middle of an asphalt desert; and we have a developer's idea of a cute place name, even the street names being mildly sickening. We live on Admiral Benbow Boulevard, so I tend to put off writing letters requiring a return address on the envelope, and I know a guy over on Long John Lane who rents a post-office box for just that reason. But it's mostly a lights-out-at-ten-on-weekdays, watch-the-late-show-Saturday-night place, and not a hell of a lot ever happens here. Little did I know, turning into my driveway, that even now a spectacular scandal was brewing, and that Fate was looking me over for one of the lead roles.

I came in through the kitchen from the driveway, and then into the living room, which is at the back of the house away from the street. My wife, Minerva, was sitting on the davenport, feet up on the coffee table, skirt up over her knees, and when she saw me looking she rolled her eyes lewdly. My name, by the way, is Samuel L. Bissell. I'm twenty-nine years old, average height, weight, looks, and color of hair. Min is twenty-five, and a hot-looking brunette. In her own opinion she's too heavy, but that isn't true. What she is is buxom, which is a hell of a lot different; she has a fine, full, womanly figure, including excellent legs, and her face is amiable and intelligent. She stood up and I kissed her, my arms around her busy tucking her skirt up under her girdle, a threadbare joke which she now expects; she'd probably be offended if I quit doing it. I said, "Lie down; I have an indecent proposal."

"What *is* an indecent proposal, anyway?"

"It's when a man asks a girl to marry him, and his fly is open."

She was sniffing my suit coat. "Goodie, you've been to the dumps," she said. Min had been against my project at first, but now she liked it. "We can work on it for a while right now, if you're not too hungry. I thought we'd eat out later; just somewhere around here." I said fine, and went back to our bedroom to change clothes.

The project was something I'd read about a couple of weeks earlier, exhibited at the Museum of Modern Art in New York. The next night I'd stopped at the dump on my way home from work, picked up whatever I could find to start my own, including a big double bedspring, and the thing had been growing ever since. Our living room opened, through sliding glass doors, onto a concrete-paved patio, and the bedspring lay at the far edge of the patio forming a sort of platform for dozens of rusting objects of junk fastened to it. They were lashed to the spring with wire, or wedged into its broken coils, or in some instances welded to it. This jungle of objects rose above the bedspring for heights varying from a few inches to over seven feet. They were odd lengths of steel such as concrete-reinforcing rods and rusted-out car mufflers and exhaust pipes; they were parts of washing machines, vacuum cleaners, various other machinery, and toys; they were wheels and cogs and odd lengths of wire; they were the glass door from a washing machine, a busted stringless tennis racket, and a large sepia photograph of a mustached man in a lodge uniform. Several hundred pounds of junk like that were fastened to the bedspring, and connected complexly to each other by a network of old fan and motor belts, sections of inner tube, ropes, and in one place, an old elastic corset.

All this was joined to a big black ½-horsepower motor, one of the few things I'd had to buy. It sat lashed to the center of the bedspring like a round black spider down in the center of the junk, and was connected to a wall socket in the living room by an extension cord across the patio. I'd run thin steel wires from its toggle switch out to the corners and edges of the bedspring, so that from anywhere near it you could just reach into that forest of junk with a hand or foot, push or pull one of the wires, and the motor would come on and the whole weird structure would begin to move.

Wheels revolved which turned belts which moved other wheels which operated cogs, shafts and eccentric gears—so that shafts rose and fell, and things wobbled, whirled, lurched, and spun. The tennis racket flapped back and forth at an old ball suspended from a string so that it passed right through the stringless frame over and over again. The mustached photograph jounced up and down, appearing and disappearing behind the glass-paneled washing-machine door. And the whole thing clattered and shook, clanked, vibrated, scraped, and banged to make the goddamnedest noise you ever heard. It was an enormous mobile, the kind of anything-goes art which is a boon to talentless people like me with a frustrated creative urge. And once it had begun shaping up Min loved it and had even worked on it herself daytimes. When it was finished and I'd found a good name for it, we were going to have a cocktail party out here, and I figured the thing would be a sensation.

Out on the patio now, in wash pants and a patterned cotton shirt, I took one of the metal disc wheels I'd brought home off its axle. Min came out with a couple of drinks, we each took a gulp, then she held the wheel on the patio cement while I punched holes near the rim with a small twelve-pound sledge and a big spike. Then I heaved up one corner of the bedspring, and shoved the other wheel, which was still on its axle, underneath the spring so that it lay on its side on the concrete. The weight of the spring held it in place, and the axle stuck up through the spring and protruded a foot or so above it. I fastened the other wheel back onto the axle, Min went into the house to find some string, and I punched a hole near the edge of each of the hub cups I'd found. Then, with short lengths of heavy string, we tied the hub caps to the wagon wheel. I cut off a narrow circle of inner tube to make a belt, and ran it from the groove of the wagon wheel to a shaft, then Min pushed down on one of the wires to the toggle switch, and the insane clanking movement began, the bedspring heaving and squeaking, and the hub caps rose like a flight of birds and fanned out into a marvelous flashing whirligig. It was a spectacularly successful addition, one of the best so far, and Min and I sat there on the pavement staring at it, sipping our drinks, turning to grin at each other, and from the corner of my eye I was watching the house next door.

Because an unexpected bonus from this contraption was that the sight of it delighted, and the sound of it frequently attracted, Janet Ebbett who lived there. She was an old friend of Min's, a college classmate at Mills, and a couple of months ago they'd run into each other at Blum's lunch counter on Union Square. Janet had just gotten a divorce and was looking for a new place to live, and since the house next door was for rent, Min suggested it to Janet. She took it, and the revival of her friendship with Min was helping her through a lousy time.

Most everything about her interested me strangely; I think I'd have had some small interest in just listening to her grocery list, item by item. For one thing, while she had no money of her own except a small monthly alimony check, she was a genuine heiress, the only one I was ever likely to know, standing to inherit some eleven million dollars from a grandfather. I'd find myself staring at her sometimes, just thinking about that. She was also a magnificently long-legged, honey-haired, good-looking girl, a confection for the eyes, and sometimes I'd find myself staring at her and thinking about that. There must have been times when Min wondered what the hell she'd been thinking of to induce this creature to move in next door.

Sure enough, my trained ears detected, above the clattering of the contraption beside us, the sound of

Janet's patio doors rolling back, and I cleverly looked the other way. This meant that Min would see her step out first and that it would be Min, not me, who invited Miss Longlegs over. "Yoo-hoo!" Min called. "Come on over!" and I started in simulated surprise, and turned, hoping Janet was wearing shorts.

She was indeed. Below a red-white-and-blue middy blouse, she was wearing white shorts with a red stripe down their splendidly brief sides, revealing, as she crossed the strip of lawn between the two patios, a spectacular length of long rounded limb whose shape would tempt a bronze Civil War general to desert the army. I waited, smiling up at Janet's face as she approached till Min glanced at me to see if I was watching Janet's legs and saw that I wasn't; then I watched Janet's legs for the rest of the way. We all said "Hi," Janet admired and exclaimed over the new addition to the mobile, and Min invited her to come along with us for supper. It seemed strange, but this good-looking heiress to eleven million bucks was often a little lonely. She'd only just been divorced, and very few of her friends knew it or even knew where she was living right now.

We ate at Sabella's, a large pleasant restaurant out on the highway. Janet went home first and, regrettably, came back with a wrap-around skirt added to her outfit, but we sat three in the front seat on the way to Sabella's, Janet in the middle. This is a seating arrangement prescribed, in this situation, by local custom and there's no use fighting it, though the tight fit, thigh against firm rounded thigh, makes it a little hard to drive, especially if you take the long scenic way there as I did.

At the restaurant we had what I think was once

called a prophetic conversation. Our waitress was a short fat woman, every movement an effort, her breathing audible, yet she was genuinely concerned with our comfort. When she set our plates down, she carefully rearranged our silverware, moved the salt and pepper shakers an inch closer to my reach, and when Min bumped her coffee cup and spilled a little in the saucer, she hurried away for a cloth and came waddling back to wipe it spotless, even drying the bottom of the cup, too, her round pink face anxious that no least drop be left. "Amazing," I said when she'd left.

Janet said, "Isn't she? Makes me feel like a child visiting a wonderfully nice aunt who's anxious that I have a nice supper. I'll be afraid to leave anything on my plate."

I said, "You're right, she's a natural-born aunt. I think I'll start some kind of agency, and she'll be my first employee; I'm going to rent her out to families who haven't got an aunt. You sign up for the service, and once a week she arrives at your house. When you answer the bell, there she'll be, smiling benignly and puffing a little from climbing the stairs. Even if you haven't got any stairs."

Min said, "In her hand, carefully wrapped in a sheet of newspaper, is a jar of what looks like home-made jelly."

"With a handwritten label," Janet said, "and sealed with paraffin."

I said, "Right. And while she'll actually arrive by cab, she'll get out half a block away, and it's to be understood that she came by streetcar—not bus, but streetcar—having to change several times, the trip taking over two hours. She visits you, listens sympathetically to your troubles, helps with the dishes, then on to the next subscriber."

"You could call the service 'Hertz-Rent-An-Aunt,'" Min said.

"Wonderful. Only let's make it 'Hertz-Rent-A-Aunt.' That gives it just the little touch of grammatical flaw that makes great advertising."

"Could you visit her?" Janet said.

"Yeah, I think so; we'll maintain a little frame house surrounded by lilac bushes in permanent bloom; probably made of plastic. You have a half-hour visit once a week at a designated time, and she hurries to the screen door when you arrive, wiping her hands on her apron, and saying, 'Lands, but it's nice to see you!' A hidden secretary checks a typed list to make sure everyone gets the right aunt, because we'll have a staff of various types sitting around in a back room somewhere. Between each visit a uniformed employee, with 'Hertz-Rent-A-Aunt' stitched on the back of his coveralls, sprays the place with an aerosol can of brown-soap-and-cookie smell."

"How about uncles?" Min said.

"Sure. We may have to call this 'Hertz-Rent-A-Relative,' because we'll have all kinds; just look through our big leather-bound books, study the eight-by-ten glossy photographs, read the rates and descriptions, and pick what you want."

"I'll take a rich uncle," Min said.

"Okay, lady; we have a fine one. Waxed mustache, panama hat, double-breasted vest piped with white braid. A rascal, a roué, a gay dog. He always arrives unexpectedly from out of town, phones, and then the excitement starts. You cancel any other engagement and hurry to get ready to meet him, because Uncle

Ben is flying on to Hong Kong in the morning. He takes you to the races in the afternoon, then to champagne cocktails in his hotel suite, to dinner at some fabulous restaurant, to a hit play, to a night club. You protest at the expense, but he laughs it away. You try to pay a check, but he simply won't allow it. Of course you get the entire bill a couple of weeks later plus a stiff rental charge for the uncle. But it's worth it; a wonderful evening on the town with your rich uncle, and ten times the fun you'd have had doing the same things on your own."

Janet said, "What about renting a husband? It looks as though I might need one soon," and something in her voice wasn't kidding.

"What do you mean?" I said.

She shrugged a little. "My grandfather's pretty sick. I found out this afternoon; my attorney phoned me."

We knew what that meant; Janet had told Min. Her grandfather's will left everything to Janet when he died, if she were married. If not, it all went to some cousins. She didn't know why; he was the kind of domineering old man who never explained anything he did and who had always tried to run other people's lives. He just thought women should be married, and that was final. I said, "Well, here's to a speedy recovery for the old boy. And a speedy remarriage for you, I guess."

Janet smiled but shook her head. "I'd be lying if I said I wouldn't like to have the family money when he dies. But meanwhile he's not running my life, or ruining it either. I'll get married when I'm ready, not before."

Somewhere or other I read that a research foundation has been established to scientifically investigate old medical superstitions. The doctors chuckled for years at the notion that spider webs applied to a cut could stop bleeding. Nonsense! Poppycock! Balderdash! But after enormous research they turned up a miracle drug that speeds up blood-clotting, and it turned out to be some stuff contained in spider webs. This kind of important new medical knowledge has been discovered often enough lately to make medicine finally realize the necessity of an all-out effort to catch up with the old ladies who've always known it, and I expect to read any day that in the treatment of sprains and bruises a significant breakthrough has just been made involving vinegar and brown paper.

Together with certain personal observations, this makes me wonder if we shouldn't quit snickering about other beliefs that have survived the ages; if it might not hurt one damn bit, for example, if the Secretary of Commerce found out just what the ancients were looking for in the entrails of sheep. Because I'm convinced that Fate regularly hands out sly little hints of what's just around the bend, if we'll only pay attention. I didn't listen though, but maybe Min caught a murmur or a nudge in the ribs. Because in the parking lot Min—explaining that Janet would be getting out first—made a particular point of getting into the car before Janet and sitting in the middle between us.

2

I WOKE up Saturday morning wondering what kind of day it was; this being the weekend, that was important. But I couldn't tell because the bedroom windows are in an idiotic little row right up under the ceiling, which ensures freedom from the terrible menace of Peeping Toms but means you can't tell what the weather is like while lying in bed. You have to stand on the arms of a chair to look outside, and the only one in the bedroom is a tall-backed rocking chair. What you do is step up onto the seat, holding onto the chair with one hand, your other arm out to the side, balancing. You don't try to stop the rocking but to control it, knees bent, the sensitive pads of the toes alert. When the rocking subsides to an irreducible minimum, you put your left foot up onto a chair arm, then sort of jump up in the air with your right leg. For a moment, your body rising, you are weightless, no pressure on the chair arm from your foot. In that moment you move your other foot to the right, it drops onto the other chair arm, and there you are in the classic posture of a bareback rider in the circus: a hand on the chair back as though gripping the reins, the other arm out to the side, gracefully balancing; knees bent, rear end thrust out elegantly. You're rocking a little wildly at that point, but if you can keep your wits and nerve, that's soon controlled, and now you can safely lift your chin to look outdoors and see what the hell it's doing, cursing all building contractors unto the seventh generation.

I wasn't ready for that yet. I wanted to enjoy the luxury of not having to get right up and the feel of the weekend stretching ahead. In the summer I generally picture the weekend—on Friday night or early Saturday, anyway—as a sort of level plain stretching off toward a distant horizon and covered with tall grass and daisies which conceal the cliff edge and sudden terrible drop onto the jagged rocks and slimy quicksand of Monday morning and Burke & Hare.

So I just lay there, pretending I was rich, and pretty soon Min began to wake up. This takes time, with her, and generally starts with her legs moving slowly up and down as though she were trampling grapes in a horizontal position. I waited and when her eyes presently opened said, "Hi, I just clocked you for a mile and a furlong in the morning workout; I think you're ready, and I've got a bundle on you." She understood no word of that and just said, "Hi," in the middle of a yawn and began to stretch. Min loves to stretch, going through some interesting variations: fists clenched up at her chest like a distance runner, her shoulder blades trying to meet; arms straight out and flapping horizontally, like a kid making angels in the snow, and maybe smacking me in the eye; then maybe one arm at a time reaching for the ceiling, fingers working, and all the while yawning and groaning in almost indecent ecstasy. Min also likes to sneeze; she's a fine sensual girl, and my advice to a young man about to marry is to find out how she stands on yawning and sneezing. I've suggested that with a box of snuff on her bedside table Min could start each day with a really awesome test series of multimegaton sneezes, yawns, trampling of grapes, moans, groans, and stretchings, and that with a recorded fife-and-drum accompaniment in the room it would be sensational.

I watched her perform for a while; when a woman's arm is outthrust rigidly her forearm actually bends backward at the elbow, a splendid thing to see. Then I lifted the covers to peek underneath, saying, "Ah, just as I suspected—a nightgown full of goodies." She rolled out of bed, with me making a grab for her, but I missed. I said, "Listen, kiddo, under California law a wife cannot refuse her husband what are known in legal parlance as his 'marital rights.' I now formally demand them, so get the hell back here."

"You're not my type."

"I'm warning you; it's illegal to refuse. I'll count to three, then I'm phoning the cops."

"I wonder what it's like out."

"Hop up and see."

Min's as good at mounting the rocking chair as I am, and she got up on the chair, balancing on the arms, waiting for the rocking to slow down so she could lift her head and look out the window. I said, "A splendid sight; you look like a Rolls Royce radiator ornament. What's it doing out?"

"Mount Tamalpais is erupting; the gods are angry. It's nice; bright and sunny." She was staring off at something, eyes narrowed. "Too bad you're not up here. Janet just came out, and she's wearing shorts."

"I prefer the view from here."

"You damn well better." Min began to get down. "She's coming over. I think something's wrong."

There was. Over coffee at our kitchen table, Min and I in our robes, Janet told us what she'd heard this morning by phone. Her grandfather had died suddenly, in a hospital on the Peninsula. They had taken him to a Palo Alto funeral home, and Janet was going down there this afternoon. I think she felt what we generally feel when someone we know, but not someone we loved, has died; a certain amount of sorrow and regret for him because his life is over, and a little awe at the mystery of it. But this was an old man, someone she'd never known at all well, and watching Janet's face, I had an idea her conscience was bothering her. So I said, "Janet, I know you have a decent feeling for your grandfather, but I don't think you have to pretend to yourself that you have no interest in his money. You have to think about it, so what are you going to do? Will you really lose it all?"

She nodded. "Yes. When I got a divorce I risked exactly what's happened. My attorney wants to talk about it, but I'm sure there's nothing to be done. He insists on coming over right away, though; he's on his way now. I asked him to come here. I thought you wouldn't mind, and I wanted you to hear what he said."

He arrived: a Mr. Wycke, pronounced Wick; a thin, fortyish man permanently welded into a suit of quiet lawyer-gray, and looking as though he never looked as though he either needed a haircut or had just had one. Min and I were dressed then—in weekend cotton dress, pants, shirt, and accessories such as shoes—and we all sat out on our patio, Min passing coffee around. Sitting in his aluminum-tubing-plastic-web chair, Mr. Wycke glanced once at the mobile, then at me, and I realized that I could read minds.

He didn't actually talk with the finger tips of one hand pressing the finger tips of the other, but he sounded like it. After expressing polite and formal regret at the passing of Gramps, he got right down to what really matters—money. He said, "Now then, Mrs. Ebbett, the important question is: are you married or are you not?"

Janet looked puzzled. "Why, I'm not. I'm divorced."

He smiled tolerantly. "That's how you would think of it, of course. Yet, this being California, you have not and will not have a final decree of divorce until a year has passed. And until that final decree is granted, the law will not allow you to marry again. How can it be said, therefore, that you are now unmarried? For if you were in fact unmarried, you would be free to marry. If, instead, you are unfree to marry, it follows that you must be married. You might well win any dispute over your right to inherit on the ground that you are still married."

"Well, yes," Janet said slowly. "I just didn't realize. I guess I *am* still married! You might even say I'm happily married, because I'm a lot happier than when my husband was around."

Min said, "That's wonderful, Janet! I'm sorry your grandfather's dead, and all that. But—"

"On the other hand," Wycke said, and we all sat back in our chairs, "the generally understood meaning of marriage is a man and woman living together in the married state, which you are not. The contention of the alternate heirs might well be that you are obviously not married in the intended meaning of the word as used in your grandfather's will. They might very well win any dispute over your right to inherit on the ground that you are not still married."

I had a quick mental picture of young law-student Wycke as a one-man debating team in law school, running back and forth across the platform taking both sides, and winning a draw decision. "And you can be sure," he was saying, "that, as things stand now, their attorneys will advise them, with some eleven million dollars at stake, to dispute your right to inherit. Win or lose, the case could drag on interminably and terribly expensively."

"Well, what should I do?"

"Don't risk such a dispute, since there is an excellent way to avoid it."

"What way?"

He leaned toward Janet, slowly shaking his finger. "This is why I hurried over here today. You must get your husband back immediately. Have him move in with you, and the decree will be invalidated. In California an initial decree of divorce is dissolved by a husband and wife merely resuming living together. You will unquestionably then, in law and in fact, be married and inherit. For undoubtedly, in that case, their lawyers will advise them not to contest. The terms of a will aren't easily set aside, and there would then be absolutely no sensible or even possible grounds on which to contest."

But long before he was finished Janet was shaking her head. "I certainly will not!" she said. "We're divorced, we're finished, and to take him back just for money, even eleven million dollars, would be—

it would be positively indecent! I'd feel like a—well, I don't know what!"

"But for *eleven m*— Look, Mrs. Ebbett, you could afford to simply give him a million-dollar settlement, once you inherit, and divorce him then."

"What an *awful* thought! Why, that's just *terrible!* Don't you think so, Min?"

"Certainly!" Min was drawn far back in her chair away from Wycke, looking down her nose at him. "What a perfectly disgusting idea."

"Why, I wouldn't come near him with a ten-foot pole!" Janet said. "Think of something else."

"There isn't anything else! Unless you do what I tell you, your cousins will certainly go to court, advancing the contention that you are in actual fact not married, and claiming the inheritance."

"Why will they? They don't know I'm divorced! Hardly any of my friends even know!"

His mental finger tips came together again, and he shrugged. "With this much money at stake, you may be sure they will investigate even the bare possibility that you aren't married. And since your divorce suit is a matter of public record, they will learn of it immediately."

Janet shook her head no. "Ebbett is only a sort of Anglicized version of Howard's name. So is Howard, for that matter. His name is actually Polish, and even I can't pronounce it and doubt if I could spell it. They don't know the name. They'll have no way to connect it to me if they see it in the records."

Wycke said, "I don't suppose they will, in that case, but it's an unrealistic hope all the same. Because with any least hope of inheriting eleven million dollars, they'll have no trouble finding attorneys and private

25

investigators aplenty willing to look into your life in every possible way, searching for some reason to contest your inheritance. I believe you and your husband had quarrels before your divorce, sometimes in public places. They were even mentioned in Herb Caen's column: 'Looks like a lot of errors, and then an out at Ebbett's Field!' So your cousins are at least aware of the possibility. And once they find that your husband is no longer living with you, it won't take them long to find out why, no matter under what name the divorce action was taken."

I said, " 'Hertz-Rent-A-Husband,' " and Wycke looked at me as though he were about to ask what I meant, then he glanced at the mobile and said nothing.

Janet thanked him for his trouble then, and we all stood up. Just before he left I reached out with my foot and turned on the mobile, and shouting into his ear, I asked Wycke if he thought I could get a patent on it. He yelled back that that wasn't his field and that I should consult a patent attorney. I asked him to recommend one, but he said he didn't know any and left. Janet left for Palo Alto then, and Min and I sat down again, watching the mobile, with Min murmuring, "I think it's terrible, just *terrible!*" Since this covered nearly everything that had happened— from Janet's divorce, her grandfather dying, the lawyer's indecent proposal, and the possibility of the cousins getting all the dough—I didn't ask what she was referring to but went into the house to fix a drink.

3

ABOUT noon on Sunday I walked
out to the patio in weekend costume—brass-studded
tan rodeo pants, white ribbed wool socks and black
mocassins, white shirt open at the collar and the tabs
buttoned down—just like a college boy, giving me
the illusion of youth and freedom. I sat down in the
shade of the house on a stretched-canvas-and-alumi-
num device which tipped me way back until my feet
were higher than my head, which was supposed to be
good for me, according to Min. I had the Sunday
paper in my lap and began feeding it into the funnel
of my mind.

I'd just finished the neurotic necessity at breakfast
of reading the first section, whimsically labeled
"news." But already the an-ulcer-is-beginning feeling
was beginning to subside, because in Bay Area papers
news stories are kept mercifully sketchy, many being
omitted entirely. As always each morning, I remembered guiltily that the *New York Times* was now
publishing a daily west-coast edition, but I pushed
the ugly thought away. I knew I'd eventually yield to
a compulsion to subscribe and read all the macabre
details of national and international news which the
local papers in their greater wisdom and restraint
generally spare us. But it hadn't happened yet, and
the scanty news out of the way, the stomach pains

subsiding and my conscience clear, I was now free to read the wonderful little foreign-datelined chronicles —what Tokyo cab drivers think of American television with Japanese soundtracks; how Brussels' teenagers have begun gilding their toenails—with which my paper keeps me abreast of what's going on in the world.

That finished, I began pouring the magazine section down the funnel, starting with a column of jokes provided each Sunday by one of America's foremost publishers. I always read them; they had the peculiar slippery quality of sliding out of my mind even before I'd finished reading them, so that I'd reach the punch line with no memory of the initial situation, a strange but pleasantly soporific effect after a week's hard work at the office. Then I took the test that showed how good a husband I was, scoring high in the "Excellent to Superior" range, and I set the section aside to show Min.

Next I began pouring in the columns, which will eventually replace news entirely out here, and a good thing. As always, I started with Herb Caen, who had a very nice Sunday p-f column—pigeons and fog. Then, in the pink section, I began the gossip column which keeps me up to date on what Sammy Davis, Jr., Jayne Mansfield, and others, including many I've never heard of, are up to. I was in the middle of that when I heard Janet call, "Hi! Good morning!" from her patio, and I hauled my feet down to the patio pavement and turned to look.

She was wearing a short skirt and very sheer nylons, a combination which in certain subtle ways is even better than the blatancy of shorts. I called, "Hi! Morning, Jan!" and beckoned her over. I thought that was clever: the sliding patio doors being open, Min would hear our exchange of greetings in the kitchen, but not seeing my gesture, would assume that Janet had come over of her own volition.

Janet walked across the strip of lawn between our houses, and I sat waiting, smiling, squinting against the sun somewhat more than necessary to hide the fact that although my face was lifted to suggest that my eyes were on her face, I was actually refreshing my memory of the entire grand length of her for future daydream reference. As she walked onto the patio, around the mobile, I said, "Hi," again and picked up the pink section to read aloud from the gossip column. "Did you know that 'Bunny Branwell bit through the ear of a middle-aged Brazilian super-markets-tycoon playboy in a Manhattan nitery the other Ayem'?"

"He had it coming to him," Janet said, and sat down on one of the plastic-web-and-aluminum chairs, crossing her legs, and by sheer indomitable pluck I kept my smiling eyes on her face. "Everything all right?" I said, and she nodded and said, "What's new? How's Min?"

"She's fine. She'll be out here in a second," I said. My cleverness this morning was awesome; it was entirely possible that Min, not knowing Longlegs was here, wouldn't be out for many long minutes. "As for what's new, I've just finished my daily briefing. At Shannon Airport a new drink craze, Irish whisky and bog water with a four-leaf shamrock embedded in each ice cube, is replacing Irish coffee among smart air-minded tourists. While fashionable Argentinians are agog over *Yanqui bezbol*, and it is said that a Little League is being organized in Buenos Aires.

What's new with you? What're you going to do about Gramp's money?" *What would you do if I walked over and nuzzled that glorious honey-colored hair?*

"Why, nothing, I guess. Except just hope I get it without any trouble from the cousins."

Pretty soon Min came out, having slipped out of her ratty blue jeans, one of my old shirts, and decayed bedroom slippers, into a pleated blue skirt, snug white blouse, nylons, and high heels. She also looked highly edible and nourishing, and I sat there, my feet healthily elevated and growing numb, glancing brightly from one to the other of this splendid pair of ladies as though I were following their nonsensical chatter, and thinking forbidden thoughts. If only it were somehow possible, if only society would come to accept the idea that in addition to Min, it would occasionally be all right if I—ah, to hell with it. I pushed aside the pink section, and under the green section found the yellow section, inserted it between me and them, and began reading the antique-car ads, wishing I had the nerve to clean out our bank account, buy a 1924 sport-model Hupmobile with disc wheels, and actually use it every day, driving to work when it rained with the canvas side curtains up.

Min was saying, "I'm completely opposed, naturally, to lying or dishonesty of any kind whatsoever. But to just sit by and let your cousins get that money is ridiculous. Why, they're not even cousins; they're only your *second* cousins!"

Janet said, "Well, of course it was entirely up to Granddad to whom he left his money, and I wouldn't dream of interfering with his wishes in any least way. But they don't *deserve* that money! And if they think I'm just going to hand it over to th— Oh, my God!" she said in an entirely different tone of voice, and I dropped my paper and turned to follow her eyes out between the two houses to the street and a blue-and-white station wagon at the curb before her house.

A woman and a man were getting out, the woman glancing all around the neighborhood even before she was entirely out of the car, and Janet said, "It's them. It's the cousins. I might have known." Then she stood up and called, "Yoo-hoo!" in a delighted tone of voice.

They saw her; she beckoned, and as they began walking toward us across the grass, I had a chance to look them over. Even allowing for the prejudice of our being on Janet's side against them, I think it's an objective fact that they were not likable people. Walking toward us, they emanated suspicion like heat waves, and above the big teeth-showing smiles their eyes searched us over like monkeys hunting lice. The woman was forty-odd, skinny, her skin deeply tanned for too many summers. But she was smart-looking; her summer dress and hat—wide-brimmed to keep the sun from showing up the lines of her face— were expensive. Her smile was garden-party polite, but her face was permanently hostile to every living soul in the world whose opinions were different from hers.

But I was positively fond of her compared to what I felt about the man who was with her; if we'd been dogs we'd have streaked across the lawn for each other's throats. He was that big, tall, wide, pseudo-athletic type, the kind that at first glance looks like a former football player. But they never are, being too wide-hipped—flab-waisted since early adolescence. I knew this son of a bitch; I'd known dozens like him; everyone has. They're affable, easy-laughing, easy-joking, in a way that can be charming till you see that it comes from never having even once in their lives perceived anything wrong with themselves. In their thirties and forties—and this one was about thirty-five—a sullenness begins showing through the charm, even a viciousness. This comes from the accumulating frustrations of a selfishness that is absolute, and they often become semi-drunks, nasty after a few drinks. I didn't really care for him.

We were standing, in a sort of meeting of the enemy chieftains, as they stopped before us, and Janet introduced us. They were a Mrs. Irene Krupp, and her brother, Jack Bailey, and I thought, *It would be Jack and not John; any guy calls himself Jack as though it were a name and not a nickname couldn't be trusted not to steal a wet cigar butt.* True to type, he was looking Min over thoroughly, and I yanked his eyes to me with, "Glad to know you, Bailey, old man," with a knife in my voice. Min glanced at me, meaning, *Cut it out, now,* and Bailey flicked me a look meaning, *I know that you know that I know that you know that we both know how things stand between us, and always will, and that goes double for me, buddy-boy,* and I returned the look, feeling good; nice and warm and mean with dislike for the bastard. It wasn't till I turned and saw the astonishment in Min's eyes that I realized what else Janet was saying.

While all these meaningful looks were going on she'd continued her introductions with, "This is my neighbor, Mrs. Samuel Bissell." Then she slid her hand possessively under my arm, saying, "And of course this is my husband, Howard. I do hope you'll call him Howie!"

I stood there, a little dazed, while they muttered responses, their eyes narrowed, studying me as closely as a guy buying a diamond in an alley. But I was able to admire the logic and simplicity of Janet's fast thinking. This unholy pair had caught her flat-footed, if you can use flat even figuratively for a girl like Janet, even referring only to her feet. Maybe I should say they caught her off-base, or with her—we'll make it flat-footed. With Gramps barely gone, they'd come rushing up from their lairs on the Peninsula on whatever off-chance might exist to find something, anything, before Janet could hide it, that would give them an excuse to contest her inheritance. And they'd almost succeeded.

But not quite. Her hand under my arm, she obviously seemed to have a husband, and now she said, "Min, darling, if you'll excuse us. . . ?"

Grinning at the startled look on my face, Min said, "Of course."

I'd recovered when we reached Janet's patio doors, remembering to step aside like a host and let the others precede me into the living room. As they did, I smiled over at Min, waved, and called pleasantly, "Tell Hertz to send the bill to me!" and she thumbed her nose at me.

For twenty minutes we sat in Janet's living room with nothing to discuss. Janet just sat back on the davenport, smiling at the pair of them pleasantly, and let them struggle with whatever they could find to offer, which wasn't much, as reason for coming here. She had a good time, and so did I. With my hands clasped comfortably back of my head, I sat on the davenport beside Janet sneering at Bailey across the room. Once I said, "Janet, love, when you sell the estate I think each of your cousins should have something from it; an ash tray, a favorite old plate, a sentimental memento of some sort. Their visit of condolence today so very soon after he passed on"— I smiled at them brilliantly—"shows how dearly they loved the old fellow."

Irene smiled back at me, and I knew how it had felt riding in a tumbrel past the eyes of the women knitting beside the guillotine. Bailey stared at me and began wetting his lips over and over. Through several seconds I thought he was not going to be able to hold back an answer, but he did. He finally swallowed whatever he'd had to say, and I mean literally; his Adam's apple moved up and down as though it were apple-bobbing time at Halloween. He sat there then, glaring at me, and my heart sang.

When they left, muttering bloodcurdling goodbyes, Janet and I stood in her front doorway, arms around each other's waist like a couple in a life-insurance ad, and Bailey bucked the car in his hurry to leave. I turned to smile down at Janet and said, "Well, dear? Where's my five and a half million bucks? Community-property law, you know," and I squeezed her waist in friendly fashion.

She quickly removed her arm from my waist and herself from my arm, saying quickly, "Let's call Min over! She'll be dying to hear all about this," so we did, and she was.

Later, when Min and I were back in our own living room, she looked at me appraisingly for several seconds, then said, "You liked that, didn't you?"

"Liked what?" I looked up from my magazine.

"You know damn well what; pretending that you and Janet—"

"Oh, maybe," I said, smiling at Min, and putting the magazine down. "She's a cute kid, and all that." I got up, walked to the davenport where Min was sitting, and sat down beside her. "Lots of things I like," I said, and got my arm around her. "But some more than others."

She said, "Stop that," but didn't move away.

"Okay, Minnie."

"And you can cut that out, too."

"Is it true that you're the only girl in the world named after a mouse?"

"I mean it now. My name is—"

"I know. But I'll bet you wouldn't mind if my name were Mickey Mouse."

"Your name is Samuel Rat. Now let me go, I have to fix lunch." And she pulled away and stood up. But she was smiling at me, and I was smiling back, and there would never be enough honey-haired blondes in the entire world to replace her little finger.

Let me explain. I really and truly, cross my heart, love Minerva, my lawful wedded wife. I would not trade her for a full-size replica of the Colossus of Rhodes carved from a single diamond. I love her in all the ways there are; she's the bee's knees. But bumbling old Mother Nature will not admit or even recognize those facts and just shut up and let me alone. She keeps murmuring in my ear, "Wouldn't it *also* be nice—wouldn't it be grand and glorious, all the Fourth of Julys since seventy-six rolled into one—to slip under the sheets with that long, lithesome, limber—" And I clap my hands over my ears,

yelling, "No, no, you old fool, I'm married! *Married,
you hear?*" And in that stupid Neanderthal voice she
says, "Married; what's that? It has no place in my
scheme, never has and never will, and—this is an
order!—I want you to sneak over to Janet's—"

There ought to be a sort of time-out. Every once
in a while a universal bell would ring and for just
an hour, a day, a night, you weren't married. When
it passed, you were married again and that hour, day,
or night didn't count, so that you'd have an absolutely
clear conscience—I'm only kidding, of course.

I just want to make it plain that it wasn't my fault;
it was Stepmother Nature who lured me into a com-
plex dream that night in which Janet's voice kept
calling, "Sam!" in an urgent, seductive whisper that
I wanted to answer but couldn't because of my better
self. Then suddenly I was awake, propped up on an
elbow in the dark, and it seemed to me that in just
the instant before I'd awakened she'd again called,
"Sam!" with still greater urgency. And now the voice
whispered desperately, "Sam, for heaven sakes, wake
up!" And I realized it *was* Janet and knew where she
was; just outside the stupid little windows up under
the eaves.

I got up, found the chair, climbed up on it, and
stood, right foot on the seat, left foot on the chair arm,
a hand lightly gripping the back, rocking at what I
estimated to be a steady thirty beats to the minute,
excellent conditions for the ascent. Then, right leg
bent, calf tensed, I leaped into the air, my groping
foot moving out to the right as it had done so many
times before. You wouldn't think darkness would
make all that difference, but it did. My foot just
passed on over that chair arm out into space, and I

felt my body following it with the rapidly increasing acceleration of a felled tree. I knew I was on my way to the floor between chair and the foot of the bed and would break both arms, my skull, and dozens of ribs, and I made a tremendous effort.

Like an Alpine climber feeling the avalanche begin under his feet, and who makes a normally impossible leap across a chasm, I shoved my left foot against the rocker arm with the strength of a stallion. The chair flew across the room and crashed into the dresser like a runaway steam roller, rattling the entire house on its foundation. And in the very instant of that crash I landed on my back on our bed with the force of a jetliner momentarily touching down in a crash landing.

My eyes were now accustomed to the faint light in the room, and as my back pressed deep into the mattress from the force of my fall, I watched Min—she'd been asleep on her stomach, and I saw her eyes pop open—rise from the mattress from the counterforce of my landing and soar on up past me. But our courses weren't parallel; I'd struck at an angle, and they intersected. And as the springs under me compressed to their limits, then shot me toward the ceiling like a trampoline, we collided in mid-air and fell back toward the bed in a thrashing tangle of pajamas, nightgown, arms and legs, and Min screamed and began to fight for her life. It was a weak scream, the tuned-down fractional yell of a nightmare; she told me much later that she dreamed a giant bird had seized her in mid-air. But as she began slugging me, I grabbed her around the upper arms and felt the swift deep inhalation I knew was the immediate preliminary to a full-fledged ear-splitter. I didn't know why,

37

but Janet's whispered cries had been unmistakably urgent with the need for secrecy, and just as Min's mouth opened to yell, I clapped a hand over it. Her teeth clamped down on my little finger, I began a shouted whisper of, "It's me, darling, it's Sam!" and after a moment I felt her relax, then she reluctantly let go of my finger.

"What in the living *hell* are you doing?" she asked, not unreasonably.

"I don't know, but Janet's here."

"*Where?*"

"Up here, Min," Janet's whispered voice said from somewhere near the ceiling.

"Oh, my God," Min said, and lay down again. "I'm still dreaming."

I got the chair upright under the windows once more, and standing only on the seat this time, I could still see the pale blur of Janet's face a foot above me on the other side of the window screen. I said, "Hi, Janet. Nice to see you again."

"I'm standing on a box on top of that wooden saw-horse, or whatever you call it, that you keep in the back yard."

"Splendid! But wouldn't it be easier to just ring the doorbell? Or even phone?"

"No, the wires may be tapped! And I couldn't ring the bell, or you might turn on a light before I could warn you."

"About what, Janet?" I said gently.

"That they're outside, watching!"

"I see," I said, knowing that in the deep middle of the night, brooding over no one might ever know what, Janet had gone insane. "Come on around; I'll let you in the side door."

"Don't turn on a light! And be very quiet."

"Okay, Jan," I said, and went around to the side of the house by the garage and let her in. She was wearing a white terrycloth robe and was barefooted.

We sat cross-legged on the bed in the darkness then, all three of us, very cozily, and I thought approvingly of the early-day Latter-day Saints and some of their curious and lamentably vanished beliefs.

Janet said, "I don't know why, but I woke up with this funny feeling. So I walked to the front of the house, peeked under a window shade"—she paused dramatically; we're all hams from birth—"and there, parked across the street, was this truck. I'm sure it wasn't there when I locked up the house earlier."

I said, "What kind of truck?"

"You know—like a sedan, only it doesn't have any windows."

"A panel truck?"

"I guess so. I watched for about five minutes, not moving the shade, and I'm sure I saw a movement in the front seat."

"Maybe it's just some guy out with a girl in the company truck and nowhere else to go."

She shook her head. "It's awfully late, even for that."

I got up, walked to the front of the house, and in the kitchen—a lot of Treasure Island houses are reversed on their lots, living rooms secluded at the back —I looked through the crack between window frame and shade. There was a Ford panel truck parked across the street, and in the light from a street lamp a dozen feet down the road I read the name painted on the panel. It said, "Bayview Rug Cleaning," and underneath that, "Mission at Fourth," and under

that "Call us for an estimate!" But there was no telephone number, no city name, and Mission and
Fourth could be streets in any town in California.

Back in the bedroom, sitting in a closet so no light
could possibly show outside, I used a pencil flashlight
to look up Bayview Rug Cleaning in both the San
Francisco and Marin County phone books. There was
none listed, and I knew that Janet was right. For
whatever reason—whatever we'd done, looked, or said
that hadn't quite been right—the cousins were suspicious. They may not even have been sure of what
they suspected, but they weren't giving up eleven
million dollars without a struggle. Outside in that
truck was a private investigator, very well paid, and
no doubt with the chance of a spectacular bonus, who
was waiting and watching to learn anything there
might be to learn, to see what he could see. I said so
to Janet and Min, then added, "And there's one
thing he *has* to see." I paused like Sergeant Friday,
waiting for someone to say, "*What's that?*"

"What's that?" Min said, knowing damn well.

"A husband leaving for work in the morning."

We were all dead silent then, the alarm clock ticking away; no one quite wanted to say the next word. I
felt sorry for Min; I could read her mind. She was
adding up the columns in a set of mental books. On
one side of the ledger, in a column headed *Virtues,* it
said, Trust in One's Husband! But in the column
opposite headed *Possible Consequences,* it said, in
red ink, Alone? At Night? With Someone Who Looks
Like Janet? Under *Virtues* it said, Loyalty to a
Friend! Under *Possible Consequences*—Friend? Or
Other Woman? But of course the books wouldn't
balance by eleven million dollars; she couldn't let

Janet lose her inheritance over a triviality. "What about the neighbors?" she said weakly. But we live on a curve of the road and there are only two houses across the street that can actually see Janet's or our house; the houses on either side are around the bend out of sight. I pointed this out gently, adding that both families across the way were on vacation, and Min nodded. "Well, then!" she said brightly, gaily. "I guess you'll have to leave from Janet's in the morning!"

We all knew this meant going over to Janet's before daybreak; there was no other way to avoid being seen crossing between the two houses. I was glad I was on the other side of the room sitting in the closet, and I didn't answer right away, to give the impression that I was weighing her suggestion while hunting alternatives. Actually I couldn't even think. Alone? At night? With Janet? What did this mean? What did I want it to mean? What did Janet . . .? What did Min . . .? What the hell was going *on?* I didn't know, but it was pretty exciting.

"Well," I said presently, as though agreement were being torn from my lips, "I suppose so. I guess that's what we'll have to do, Janet." Do what? Double, triple, and quadruple entendres swirled through my brain. "Okay," I said with brisk making-the-best-of-it finality, and I got up from the closet floor decisively before anyone could have second, less-interesting thoughts, "I'll do it. Come on, Janet. I'll see you home."

"She can make it home by herself," Min said, even more decisively. "It's not far, and the fewer people flitting back and forth, the better for Janet."

I let Janet out the patio doors at the back of the

41

house and came back to bed. Min was so far over on her side she'd fall out of bed if she sneezed, and her back was squarely to me. "I've set the alarm for five-fifteen," she said coldly, as though all this were my fault. "It doesn't start getting light till after five-thirty. Now let's try to get some sleep."

"Right!" I said heartily, and as I settled down I muttered, "Hell. Five-fifteen. What a nuisance." But Min didn't move or say a word, and I knew I hadn't quite carried conviction.

At five-fifteen, shot out of sleep by the alarm like a man from a cannon, I staggered around the bedroom with my pencil flashlight, getting out shorts, shirt, tie, suit, shoes, toilet articles, wallet, keys, clean handkerchief. It was Min's idea that I ought to get dressed here; I'd be leaving for work in only two hours, she said. But I pointed out that I always take a shower in the morning, that I'd also have to shave, brush my teeth, and comb my hair, so what was the point in my dressing now? She couldn't think of an answer she was willing to make, though I felt she was trying, and just before five-thirty I left. If you think it isn't a weirdly confusing feeling to kiss your wife goodbye and then sneak through the dark over to the home of a beautiful divorcee in your pajamas and robe, carrying your clothes over one arm, shoes in the other hand, and wearing a Homburg hat—try it, buddy; just try it sometime.

As we'd arranged, Janet had opened her sliding patio doors a foot or so, the floor-length drapes drawn. I stepped inside, but with my arms full I couldn't find the part in the drapes. They were made of some kind of heavy hairy stuff that felt like burlap, and as I tried to fight through them they kept dragging across my chin, because I had to keep my head tilted back to keep the damn things from brushing my hat off; my chin was scraped nearly raw before it finally occurred to me to crawl under them. Then, hat still on, shoes in one hand, clothes over the other arm, I crept out from under the drapes on my knees and elbows and paused in this attitude of Mohammedan prayer to look hopefully around for Janet. But the absolute stillness that filled this pause was unmistakable; it was the distinctive living silence felt only in a house whose every other occupant is sleeping, far away and behind closed doors.

There was no pillow on the davenport, and I couldn't wrinkle up the clothes I had to go to work in. There were three cushions on the davenport, and I had a choice between using them all to lie on, stretched out at nearly full length, or of using one of them propped against the arm as a pillow. I can't sleep without a pillow, so presently —huddled in a thin nylon robe, and shivering a little—I lay down with my head on one cushion and the rest of me squeezed, knees under chin, onto the four-foot combined length of the other two. Lying there, my emotions were a kind of stew made up of equal parts of physical discomfort, irritation, and disappointment, and flavored with enormous relief, and I thought about Min and wished I were in bed directly and snugly beside her where I belonged.

Around six I finally dozed off; I'd glanced at my watch in the sick white light of dawn a few minutes earlier. About forty seconds later the birds began, abruptly and all at once, on signal from some bird-brained leader. Who says birds sing? They don't sing; it's the most raucous, demented sound in the entire repertory of addle-pated Mother Nature, and the damned ignorant birds kept it up till six-thirty. At seven the hall door leading to the other end of the house popped open, and Janet popped in, radiant and lovely with a night's healthy sleep. Her hair was tied entrancingly up off her slim lovely neck with a yellow ribbon of very much the same honey shade, and she exactly filled an olive-colored knitted dress in a way that might very well have driven me mad with desire if I hadn't been so tired and cold and had a pulsating headache, apparently from an ax blow directly over the eyes. "Good morning, Sam!" she said, walking briskly toward me, all but rubbing her hands with *joie de vivre*. I was struggling up into a bent and huddled posture on the edge of the daven-port, trying to smooth down my hair with my hands or to cover my face, I wasn't sure which. "Oh, I should have remembered to put out a blanket!" Janet exclaimed, stopping beside the davenport. "I was so worried and frightened when I got home that I just didn't think. I hope you weren't cold?"

"No, of course not," I mumbled, peering up and out at her from between my fingers; it had turned out that, remembering how I look without much sleep, I was trying to cover my face.

"Now, then!" she said briskly, gathering up my clothes and things from the chair on which I'd left them. "You can go shower and shave, and I'll put these in the spare bedroom; you can dress in there." Walking toward the hall with my clothes, she said over her shoulder, "You could have slept in the spare bedroom, you know," as though reproving me for some foolish stubbornness in refusing.

But the shower water was nice and hot, and I

warmed up and woke up and began thinking about breakfast. I looked forward to it, not only because I'd been awake for nearly the last hour and a half and was starved, but because this would also be breakfast across the table from Janet. No matter what the reason and however innocent, there's something a little exciting, almost risqué, about having breakfast alone with a good-looking woman, and I felt it was a small reward I deserved for what I'd suffered. By the time I was shaved and dressed, ready to walk out to the kitchen and claim my reward, I felt fine except that I'd forgotten to bring socks.

There's a special unpleasant feeling about putting shoes on bare feet, and I couldn't go to work without socks anyway. So I walked out to the kitchen fully dressed, including tie and suit coat, but barefooted. I can see how that might be a mildly amusing sight, and that Janet might smile, but I didn't think it was all that funny; the hands on hips, the head thrown back, the pealing laughter. When she quieted down a little I suggested it might be helpful if she'd go over to my place and get a pair of my socks from Min.

Carefully keeping her eyes off my feet, and yet not looking me in the eyes either—sort of sighting past my cheekbone—she said, "What if he's still watching from the truck? He'll see me crossing the lawns."

"He undoubtedly *is* watching; that's why he's here. But you could perfectly well be borrowing some sugar or something. Take a cup along."

She left, and I sat down at the kitchen table with the morning paper to wait. The big story was that Mayor Christopher was favorably disposed toward a proposal to sell part of Golden Gate Park to a subdivider. He pointed out to the "do-gooders" who objected that the park was obviously too big, since there weren't enough police to patrol it at night without increasing the city budget. Replacing some part of this area with high-rise "luxury" apartments would not only help reduce crime, therefore, but would "broaden the tax base," increasing city revenues so that either the police force could be enlarged or, if that were no longer necessary because crime in the park had been effectively reduced by decreasing the size of the park, the tax rate could be lowered, and only the "bleeding hearts" could find anything wrong with *that*. Then I read Abigail Van Buren. A man had written her for advice, his letter said, because his wife insisted on keeping her large poodle in bed with them at all times. He was fond of animals, but this not only made sleeping uncomfortable so that he was tired most of the time, his work suffering, but at certain times the dog would invariably begin to bark. His wife didn't seem to mind, but it tended to upset him. "Abby, what shall I do?" he said. "I love my wife and dog, but this spoils some of our most tender moments." She advised him to consult his pastor, of the church of his choice, she added generously, and I wished I could hear his answer. The moronic Giants had kicked one away to the Mets yesterday, and I read the sickening details in the green section. Suddenly I remembered to look at my watch and found I had to leave in six minutes.

I jumped up, and with a rueful twisted smile and a gallant bow of defeat toward my house and the wily Minerva, I began hunting for coffee and sugar and found a jar of instant coffee after only three minutes of hunting through every cupboard and drawer in that goddamned kitchen; I never did find the sugar. There was no time to boil water, so I made a cup of coffee with some fairly warm water directly from the faucet, though I couldn't get it to dissolve very well. I was standing there in my bare feet forcing down this devil's brew—the only *lumpy* coffee I've ever had in my life—when Janet finally blew in again, all gay and laughing, holding a rolled-up ball of socks out to me in the cup she'd carried, which she seemed to think was funny as hell. "Goodness, just look at the time!" she said, and yanked open a drawer, grabbed a frying pan, swung to the refrigerator, and snatched out some bacon. "I just couldn't get away, Min's so full of chatter and jokes. She simply *insisted* I have coffee and toast with her. Is she always like that in the morning?"

I had put down my cup and was standing on one foot pulling on a sock. "Always. Sometimes the morning just drifts by on gossamer wings, and I never get to work at all." I couldn't quite get the sock over my heel and was losing my balance and had to start hopping around. "Never mind the bacon," I said. "I'm not a bit hungry." And since I had to hop anyway, and was short of time, I hopped on out of the kitchen and down the hall toward the bedroom and my shoes.

4

$\mathcal{S}$TANDING at the dresser mirror, working on the angle of my Homburg—there's a certain devil-may-care tilt I just couldn't seem to find this morning—I finally gave up, jammed it on, and stood looking at myself. The crown was dented, the brim touched my ears so that I had no forehead, there were circles under my eyes, and my tongue was coated —just to complete the picture, I stuck it out—with the living spore of deadly nightshade, and I fell to brooding. Damn it to hell, if I couldn't have a night's sleep, a mouthful of breakfast, or even a decent cup of coffee, and if it was Monday morning and I was on my way back to captivity at Burke & Hare—and I certainly was—then I deserved *something*, didn't I? Otherwise where was the joy, the meaning, the *purpose* of life? It didn't all just happen, did it? Anyway, I had no choice about it; I *had* to kiss Janet goodbye at the front door now. It's what her husband would naturally *do,* I was forced into it, and besides, it was Min's idea that I come over here in the first place.

Turning toward the hall outside the bedroom, I was debating whether it had to be the quick suburban peck for authenticity or if I could linger over it, and I had a quick idiot picture of myself bending Janet backward in the doorway like Rudolph Valentin—a horn tapped, and just ahead, at the end of the hall, the front door stood open. Outside it a car motor was idling, and when I looked out at the driveway Janet sat waiting in her black Thunderbird convertible, with the top down, wearing a smart-looking car coat with a turned-up collar. "Come *on*, you'll be *late!*" She beckoned. "I have some shopping to do, and I'm riding in with you."

I drove, and it was a glum ride, my stomach growling all the way in like a broken muffler. Janet explained, at what seemed like unnecessary length, that she had to get a dress and accessories for the funeral because she wanted to look nice, and would spend the day in the city and give me a ride home. I said, "Oh," and even that was an effort because I'm just not a morning person, and I've often wondered how and when they took over the world. It must have been in the morning when the rest of us were asleep; those who, like me, would function best if only the day began around three in the afternoon. Instead, we're forced into an unnaturally early life, and until about ten-thirty I run almost entirely on conditioned reflexes; my brain doesn't really take over the ship, yawning and stretching, till after lunch.

No one followed the Thunderbird into town, as well as I could tell. The panel truck had still been parked across the street from Janet's, someone spying on us through a tiny hole in the body, I was sure. But I never once saw it in the rear-view mirror, although in the Monday-morning I-couldn't-stand-the-bus-today-of-all-days highway commuter traffic we could have been followed by an army tank without my seeing it. In the city, though, I took California Street across to Montgomery, and there was nothing at all behind us.

In front of the office I pulled over to the right-hand curb, and one of our stenographers was just turning into the building entrance, and she nodded and smiled at me, looking Janet over. The conditioned reflexes were in full charge, the captain sodden in his bunk, and my brain said that she'd think this was my blond mistress driving me to work after a night of debauch and that she'd blab it all over the office. Then I realized that there was no reason why she shouldn't assume that this was my wife. As I was puzzling that out, someone on the sidewalk said, "Morning, Sam," and Mr. Burke was standing beside the car, smiling down at Janet. He's a portly, handsome, lively old boy with thick, wavy white hair, who liked Janet's looks just fine; she sat practically at his feet, her hair resplendent in the sun, smiling gorgeously up at him. To my sluggish morning mind she seemed surrounded by an almost visible aura of guilty need-to-conceal-the-truth, and I quick-wittedly said, "Janet, this is my boss! Mr. Burke, my wife, Janet!" It wasn't till I'd walked clear around the front of the car, congratulating myself, that it occurred to me that there had been no reason why I couldn't have simply introduced her as a neighbor who'd given me a lift.

It was going to be a bad day, I could see, and I couldn't even go around the corner to the cafeteria for a life-giving roll and coffee. When Burke finally let go Janet's hand—I was afraid he'd hang on till she got gangrene—Janet said goodbye to him, entrancingly, called, "See you tonight, Sam. I'll pick you up here at five-thirty," and I had to walk into the building with Burke, matching stride for brisk stride, a song on my lips, and glad it was Monday with a whole wonderful week of work ahead.

Upstairs we walked under the four-foot glass transom on which Burke & Hare is spelled in gilt script, and I noticed that underneath this today, in smaller invisible letters, it said, *Abandon all hope, ye who enter here,* and I did, then joined Mr. Burke in greeting Grace, the receptionist, with glad little cries. In my own office, I closed the door, hung up my suit coat, yanked open my top desk drawer, and took out the manila folder of important-looking papers I kept for this purpose, spread them out on the desk top, added a pencil for verisimilitude, wadded up a ball of paper and threw it on the floor for further realism, then lighted a cigarette, and laid it on the ash tray for the convincer. I turned to head down the back stairs to the cafeteria. The phone rang, conditioned-reflex picked it up and answered, and Mr. Burke's secretary, Rose-Marie, said, "Morning, Sam. There's a Nesfresh meeting in the conference room in five minutes; emergency. Can you make it?"

This is one of the questions with only one answer that are asked around the place to foster our illusions of being sturdy independent artisans with a precious heritage of freedom, and I said, "Nothing but an assignation with you in the stock room could keep me from it," the kind of answer more or less expected from the copy or art department. Then I phoned Comet and ordered coffee and Danish to be delivered right away to Sam Bissell at Burke & Hare in the conference room, adding hopelessly, "It's a matter of life and death. Please rush it," and picked up my coat again.

I might as well confess that B&H, as they are known in the trade, is an advertising agency and that I am employed there as a copywriter. This means I'm supposed to think up clever advertising for our clients, and sometimes I do. That parade of little animated stomachs you've probably seen on television advertising "BELS for the belly" was my idea. They parade around in shifting formations, eventually spelling out BELS, to the tune of "March of the Wooden Soldiers," and carrying little picket-like signs reading, "It's goodbye burps, 'cause BELS ring the bell" and "End acid agony, bring out the BELS!" and so on. As they march, they ring little handbells and sing to the music. But instead of singing, "The toyshop doors are closed up tight, and all the toys are ready for the night," these little stomachs, which are terrifically cute—Art Blatchford, our art director, did a great creative-design job with them—they sing, "When liver bile doesn't flow just right, BELS for the belly make the world seem bright!" This commercial tied for second place last year in the Better Broadcasting Public Service Awards, and I got a plaque to hang in my office and a memo from Mr. Hare congratulating me.

Getting into my coat now, I turned to the plaque for inspiration. It's a plate-sized bronze disc (actually plastic, but so skillfully bronzed it fools everyone) mounted on a panel of simulated ebony, and it shows a muscular arm pounding a sword, inscribed *Sales*, with a big sledge labeled *Truth*. My name and so on is engraved on a little plate just below this. But looking at this splendid testimonial to my past ingenuity only proved to me that my brain was dead now, and I opened my desk drawer, got out my emergency pipe, and dropped it into my coat pocket.

I don't actually smoke a pipe; I haven't even got any tobacco. But I've discovered that what would otherwise be an obviously stupid Sam Bissell, eyes nearly closed in sleep, no thought in his head, no sensible word to say, is transformed by a pipe held near the jaw. With no other change, the narrowed eyes now suggest concentration, the empty, unfocused stare suddenly seems to be looking far beyond this little meeting, the dumb silence becomes thought.

This can carry me through two-thirds of a morning meeting without having to say a word, but of course the wisdom suggested by this pose eventually has to be demonstrated. What I do, after a while, is to begin slowly shaking my head. This is obviously not at what anyone else has said or is saying, since my eyes are looking out past the walls, but at my own thoughts. When everyone looks at me, I start shaking my head a little more emphatically, as though trying to drive off a gnat-like cloud of merely clever ideas, and I cut to the core of the problem with, "This is no time for cleverness. This is *serious*—and it's time to return to fundamentals." Not only is that hard to dispute; it tends to give an air of solidity to whatever threadbare idea I can produce, and what I generally urge, spacing my words, is, "good, plain, solid, old-fashioned testimonials." Time it right—maybe after several new ideas have been kicked apart—and nearly everyone is likely to go for it. It often cheers everyone up and they get downright enthusiastic, because the meeting's been going on for some time and they're tired of it; because it *isn't* new and fresh, so no one has to gather his wits to attack it; and because it's so tried and true, so utterly *safe,* that no one's neck goes under the ax for okaying it. It's the new ideas that are dangerous and hard on the nerves. I can't work this too often, of course, but used sparingly, it has actually enhanced my reputation. I'm more than merely clever; I'm solid. I keep the pipe for emergencies, and this was one.

Mr. Burke laid down the problem, sitting in silver-haired authority at the head of the big conference-room table on which, one Christmas party, rumor has it, Rose-Marie was promoted to the job of Mr. Burke's secretary. Art Blatchford, the art director, was there; Dan Fineburg, our copy chief; Peter Van Freiling, the Nesfresh account man; and Walter Kristoffersen, our production man. "We got troubles," Mr. Burke said humorously, then he frowned and shook his head to show this was really no laughing matter. "Mr. Nurdlinger got back from a retreat this morning."

I actually winced and felt for my pipe to make sure it was there. Mr. Nurdlinger hasn't had a vacation in years, as he often remarks; he simply hasn't the time. This makes all the Nesfresh egg executives who *do* take vacations feel guilty about them, and it also leaves them wide open to the suspicion that there are things in their lives almost as important as selling Nesfresh eggs. But Mr. Nurdlinger is so busy with the incessant daily demands of the business that he's often forced to take little "retreats," as he calls them. This means forcing himself to get off someplace where he can devote himself completely to large-scale Nesfresh thinking. In the winter he generally retreats to a little place built especially for the purpose, at a large tax saving, at Palm Springs. At other times he often goes to a little town so small, he says, that there is nothing to do *but* think about Nesfresh, about fifteen miles from Las Vegas. Whenever he comes back from a retreat he demonstrates how much harder and deeper he's been thinking than anyone else, and life at Nes-fresh and B&H is hell for a while.

"He phoned Peter this morning, wasn't it, Pete?"

"Six-thirty A.M. From the airport. I met him at his office at seven-thirty; he didn't even go home. All his own people were already there."

"Go ahead."

"Well"—Pete looked around at the rest of us; he hated to say this—"he's bounced the Nesfresh board."

Art Blatchford groaned and covered his face with his hands, elbows on the table.

"Gave his people hell for okaying it and us hell for suggesting it."

A yard-long miniature of the new billboard for Nesfresh eggs was thumbtacked to the big cork mat that covered most of one wall, and we all looked up at it. It was a huge color photograph of two eggs resting on their smaller ends, and each egg had a humorous face drawn on it. The first egg, on the left, had a girl's face with a Cupid's-bow mouth in red and with long paste-on eyelashes and a pink paper hat. The other egg was a man, his black India-ink hair parted in the middle, and with a paste-on paper collar. Above their heads were speech balloons. The girl egg, her eyes flirtatiously indignant, was saying, "Fresh!" while the boy egg was replying, "No—Nesfresh! And quit egging me on!"

Art lifted his head from his hands to look up at the billboard. He'd done the color photography for this himself and was proud of it; he's actually a fine photographer, doing all the agency's work, mostly with a Leica, and he even does some outside work for some of the studios. "What's wrong with it?" he said. "Just tell me what's wrong with it!"

Peter shrugged apologetically. "Mr. Nurdlinger says it's silly."

Everyone was quiet for a few moments then, and I got out my pipe; I had about ten minutes' grace now. This was the billboard that was to have been painted, beginning this morning, in about a dozen choice locations in San Francisco. If they got a good response, they'd be lithographed then and put up all over northern California. Rent on these choice locations was very expensive, and it had begun this morning; within minutes we had to produce a brand-new idea, one that Peter was sure he could sell to Mr. Nurdlinger, and one that could be completely produced today, ready to turn over to the paint crews tomorrow. And I had to think of it.

This would ordinarily have been the copy chief's worry, but I'm considered chief trouble shooter on the Nesfresh account because of a memo I wrote when I was still new at the agency. I simply suggested that prospective customers would be more likely to realize that Nesfresh is supposed to mean fresh from the nest—if we spelled it *Nest-fresh*. It was a very cogent, closely reasoned, four-page memo quoting leading semanticists, T. S. Eliot, an editorial in *Advertising Age,* and the result of a research survey I'd conducted myself among three girls in the typists' pool, all but one of whom preferred Nest-fresh. It created quite a stir at the client's; they had a couple of meetings on it themselves and then invited all the agency brass, and me, to a joint meeting. We had the art department make up an alternate line of dummy egg cartons, shipping crates, point-of-sale material, newspaper and magazine ads, and miniature billboards, all with the proposed new spelling. It took our artists all weekend, working nights, too, but they made it in time, and I think the client was impressed. We spread it all out on their board-room table, along with counterparts using the old spelling, and had a two-and-a-half hour meeting during which we studied the exhibits, shifting them around and narrowing our eyes, discussing them, making notes. Once Mr. Burke got up, walked slowly to a window, and stared down at the street for a minute or so, everyone watching him. Then, sort of to himself, testing it out, thinking hard, he said, "*Nes*fresh . . . *Nest*-fresh." Then he reversed it: "*Nest*-fresh . . . *Nes*fresh." He did that three or four times, absolutely unconscious of where he was for a moment, then he turned around slowly, staring over our heads, and did it again. He sort of came to then, blinking a little, and glanced all around the table, grinning in rueful amusement at how wrapped up he'd gotten in the problem—he has a very boyish, engaging grin—and sat down again.

For a while, then, the discussion got off onto whether, if we did change to Nest-fresh, the *f* should be capitalized or not. But after about forty minutes Mr. Nurdlinger suggested we ought to stick to fundamentals, and we got back to the main issue.

When the meeting finally broke up, three of the six board members seemed to like the new version, as far as we could tell, and the other three didn't seem to, we thought. (Though it turned out later, back at the agency, that none of us agreed on which three was which.) But Mr. Nurdlinger himself didn't say what he thought, so Mr. Burke suggested a survey, and —it was five forty-five—everyone agreed.

We did a full-scale fifteen-thousand-dollar job then, three hundred and seventy-five housewives, representing a cross section of the country economically, politically, religiously, age-wise, and geographically, being interviewed in depth. This means hour-long questionnaire interviews, conducted by trained psychiatrists, to get at the subjects' *real* feelings on the question, neither Nesfresh, Nest-fresh, or the subject of eggs at all, for that matter, ever being actually mentioned. The questions—a hundred and forty-four of them, many in three and four parts—were concerned with the subjects' childhoods, states of their marriages, their fears, their hopes, their dreams. (There's a new outfit that hypnotizes them, but we're afraid they're charlatans.) These questionnaires are later interpreted by the psychiatrists, but in this instance, they said, the results were inconclusive. They almost seemed to suggest that the women didn't much care one way or the other, but the report pointed out that because eggs have obvious deep-seated symbolic significances, their preferences were so buried it would take full-scale analyses to reach them, which they offered to do for seventy-five thousand dollars, but the agency decided against recommending that to the client.

So there was no way to decide the question, and a couple of months later, when he got back from a retreat in Hawaii, Mr. Nurdlinger said he'd thought it out, and that they had hundreds of thousands of dollars already invested in the old familiar spelling, and that it could be potentially disastrous to change —which we all instantly recognized as sound hard-headed thinking. But he added that even though my suggestion hadn't been adopted, it was the kind of fresh avant-garde thinking the account needed, and ever since I've been the white-haired trouble shooter on Nesfresh.

I sat there now, pipestem along my jawbone, while Art Blatchford complained to Peter that the art department was already overloaded with rush jobs and that he couldn't possibly take an artist off anything to work on a new board for Nesfresh, while Dan Fineburg complained to Peter that if he couldn't get an okay that would stick, the copy department couldn't bail him out forever, and while Walter Kristoffersen complained to Peter about the fuss Foster & Kleiser, the billboard company, were going to raise about a last-minute complete change in copy. All this was routine, which Peter expected, and when everyone was finished they all turned to me for the solution.

I'd really tried to think. (Hand holding up big newspaper; headline: NESFRESH MEANS EGGSTRA FRESH! Albert Einstein, Bertrand Russell, Immanuel Kant, Plato, all smiling. *Eggheads agree; Nesfresh means fresh, fresh,* FRESH! Scientist holding up test tube, Nesfresh carton on lab table. *Scientific tests* PROVE—*51.78% bigger, yellower, smoother yolks!*) But I couldn't think of a thing.

"Well, Sam," Mr. Burke said, "what do you think?"

I continued to stare off toward wider horizons and tried to rub the bowl of my pipe thoughtfully along the side of my nose, which is something I often read about, but I couldn't figure out how to do it so that the stem didn't stick out ridiculously. It occurred to me to run the stem through my hair, which I did, and I had the feeling it was producing a new effect. "I think this," I said slowly and solemnly, then stopped, stared off at New York, and counted silently to a hundred by tens, running the pipestem through my hair. Then I had a minor inspiration. "I think Mr. Nurdlinger is right," I said, which shook them; the possibility had never occurred to them or to me, either, till then. I nodded at the miniature billboard up on the wall—my idea. "That's clever," I said, "damned clever. The art work is brilliant, the production flawless. When Nesfresh has moved up to a stronger competitive situation in, say, six months or a year from now, I think this board will be exactly right and that Mr. Nurdlinger will agree. Just now, though, he's absolutely right; this is no time for cleverness . . ."

They were all willing enough to nod when I finished, but they had questions. "What kind of testimonials?" Mr. Burke said. "There's no time to get clearances from celebrities."

I hadn't thought that far, but Dan Fineburg fielded the ball. "You don't want celebrities for a local product like eggs; use ordinary Bay Area people. People who might actually use Nesfresh eggs, for all we know. You know, *believable*. Mr. and Mrs. Joe Blink, Geary Boulevard, San Francisco, say, 'We love Nesfresh eggs at our house because they're always bigger, better—"

"That's not actually true," Mr. Burke said apologetically, and when Dan looked baffled, he said, "What I mean is, I don't know if we could get away with—"

Dan shrugged. "Mr. and Mrs. Blink say, 'Nesfresh eggs always *seem* bigger, better, fresher!' "

"Fine," said Mr. Burke.

"It'll take time to rig up a kitchen set," Art Blatchford said, "unless one of the studios has one set up."

I had to get out of here; I was desperate for coffee. "A kitchen's too obvious, Art. Show them anywhere but. Waiting in line at the movies, looking in a store window. Outdoor, inquiring-reporter-type shots. Fake them up to look honest and real."

"Candid billboards," Pete Van Freiling said then. "I think Nurtsy will go for it."

Art said, "It'll help the candid idea if we paint them black and white direct from the photograph, no color at all. They'll really stand out; the other boards are all color-happy. And you'll make up some production time."

"I think we've got it, then," Mr. Burke said. "We'll still need clearances, though, won't we? Whoever we use."

But Dan said, "Use agency people, one of the girls in the office and her husband, or something," and that wrapped it up. Art said he could take his shots today, develop them tonight and make up some miniatures, and Pete could have them at Nurdlinger's office for him to choose from first thing in the morning; he'd start a man on the lettering as soon as I could get copy to him. I said I'd get right on it, would have it in an hour, and on the way back to my office I wondered if I shouldn't actually start smoking a pipe.

My coffee and roll were on my desk in a gray cardboard box together with a bill for sixty-five cents from Comet, which Grace, the receptionist, had paid for me. The coffee was so cold you could have cut it up for fudge, and the Leek-Pruf carton it came in was disintegrating so that the roll beside it was soaked and soggy. I got the whole mess over the wastebasket just as it burst, and a little coffee bomb hit the bottom of the basket and exploded. But three minutes later I was at the cafeteria, and ten minutes later I was drinking hot coffee and eating bacon and scrambled eggs that tasted so good they could only have been Nesfresh.

The day improved. I had lunch with Art Blatch-ford, then we poked around a magic-trick store down on Market Street. They had a line of obscene greet-ing cards, and we each picked one out to mail to our wives. After lunch I worked for about an hour, until two-thirty, on a package insert for Cheez-Krisps. It was supposed to persuade women that not only were they delicious at cocktail time, they were also a grand taste treat for the entire family at breakfast, a nau-seous thought. Then I got out my important-looking-papers file and, carrying it under one arm, made sev-eral social calls on fellow employees who also under-stood how to look busy while killing time, and Larry Boling and I worked out a new batting order for the Giants.

At five-thirty, a Monday survived and my metabo-lism steadily climbing toward high tide, I felt fine leaving the office, and the sight of Janet in her Thun-derbird parked next to the fireplug in front of the office didn't make me feel any worse. It was warm; she had her car coat off, and there wasn't a stitch to spare in the knit dress that clung lovingly, as who could blame it, to every splendid curve and hollow of that remarkable figure. To the rest of drab woman-kind walking by on Montgomery Street, she was as Macy's to the village store, and when she saw me and smiled and waved, every man walking past looked at her, then at me, cursing me with his eyes, and I swaggered to the car, spurs jangling, the great plume of my hat insolently curved, hand on the jeweled hilt of my sword. Janet began shifting over out of the driver's seat, and I walked around the car—all of Montgomery Street for blocks either way and many stories up motionless and staring in envy—and slid in under the wheel.

Skirts are hard to modestly control in a Thunderbird, sliding across the seat especially, and I didn't start up right away but sat smiling fondly down at Janet and those amazing long legs, and if the Statue of Liberty had legs and a skirt like Janet's, immigration to the States would have sent the population past six hundred million. Politely I inquired how her shopping had gone and sat listening in fascination to her answer—she had bought a dress; it had to be altered; she'd pick it up tomorrow— and I could have sat there nodding and smirking for hours. Had I really been alone even a part of the night with this abundant supply of womanhood, without pounding my chest with both fists and bursting through her bedroom door howling in berserk lust? Could metabolism actually sink that low without rigor mortis setting in? A cab honked behind me, and I finally had to look to the front and pull away from the curb.

Driving across the bridge, the radio on to a marimba-rattling Latin orchestra—Edmundo Ros, I think—I discovered that by pressing the gas pedal in time to the music, the car bucked slightly in the same regular beat, swaying us back and forward in exact rhumba rhythm. It was a delightful sensation, which I advise everyone to try, and until the record stopped we did it halfway across Golden Gate Bridge, my hand up at my right ear, wrist and outspread fingers waggling as we rhumbaed sitting down, Janet's delighted laughter pealing like harem bells in my ears. Little cotton wisps of the first evening fog were streaking across the bridge past the windshield and our faces; the wind whipped at us invigoratingly and excitingly; we were laughing at anything, and Frank Sinatra came on, singing, "If I could be with you one hour tonight." I glanced at Janet, and after an instant she looked quickly away, and in just that instant it came to me that if I had to leave from Janet's house this morning, I sure as hell had to go back there tonight.

5

I was leaning forward looking out the windshield as we came around the bend in our road, and the panel truck across from Janet's was gone. I was pretty sure the investigator, convinced of Janet's marital status, had left for good—if there had ever really been one at all, which I was beginning to doubt. But I continued leaning forward, driving slowly, staring out the windshield, but now I was looking up, searching the hills across the street. When Janet asked what I was doing, I nodded up at the hills. "That's where I'd be if I were a private eye hired to do you out of eleven million bucks; lying hidden up there in the weeds somewhere, watching every movement in and out of your house through high-powered binoculars." I swung into her driveway, set the hand brake, and turned off the motor. Janet was frowning and looking worried, and I pulled the key case from the ignition and opened my door. "'Fraid I'll have to go in with you, Janet; no help for it," I said like the British subaltern volunteering to parachute behind the lines, and Janet nodded, opening her door, the tight-lipped colonel accepting the sacrifice because there is no alternative. I walked around the back of the car, and then—what is there so insidiously seductive about following a woman toward a locked door, the key to which you hold in your hand?

"We'llhavetoletMinknowyou'rehereshe'llbewondering," Janet said the instant we stepped inside, and walked on to the kitchen at the back of the house. I stopped at the extension phone in the hallway. I _did_ have to let Min know I was here; she'd probably heard the car in the driveway. So I phoned, told her where I was and why, expecting the same reasonable acceptance of this inescapable necessity as I'd had from Janet. But Min didn't say a word; she just stood there listening. I knew because I could see her; I could see her face and feel the chill coming over the wire, extra services I was sure the telephone company would include in my next bill in revenge for my not buying a Princess phone and for certain remarks in my dossier about all-digit dialing. The result—I knew this but couldn't seem to shut off the words—was that I went on at more and more elaborate length and persuasive detailing. Soon I realized my voice had taken on the special overhearty, jocular tone of the man who stops for a drink after work, gets to talking with this girl at the bar, buys her a drink, and is now phoning his wife that he may be a little late.

After a while Min said, "You really think all this caution is necessary?"

I chuckled tolerantly. "Well, I suppose with eleven million bucks at stake we can't blame Janet for being a little overcautious."

That was hard to answer, and after a little pause Min said, "Well. All right." Then with one quick blast of the raygun she melted me. "Don't stay too long," she just couldn't keep herself from adding in a tiny, wistful, lonesome voice, and she had me; I just held out my wrists and the marriage bonds clicked back into place.

"Okay, darling," I half whispered into the phone, meaning both words, and hung up. Down the hall Janet came out of the kitchen with two drinks and saw me at the phone.

"Should you have phoned?" she said worriedly, when I got to the living room. "They might be tapping the wires."

"I doubt it," I said, though I didn't know why; maybe they were, for all I knew. "Anyway, it's better than wigwagging from the rooftop." I took one of the drinks and drank half of it down on the spot.

We sat on opposite sides of the living room, sipping our drinks, smiling at each other frequently with all our teeth and with not a hell of a lot to say. Snaggle-toothed Mother Nature stood just behind my chair wearing a ragged black cloak and a tall peaked hat, whispering, "Wow! Oh, boy! Just look at that! Go on over to the davenport, sonny, and sit down next to her, sort of casually. *Male and female*—there is no other law!" But with Min's plaintive little voice still sounding in my other ear, I was able to ignore that, and if there'd been an underground tunnel connecting the two houses, I'd have been glad to trot briskly along it back to Minerva the Magnificent. Believe me, if there were a statue of *her* in New York Harbor, the incoming population wouldn't exactly fall off, either. You say anything against Min, by God, and you got *me* to reckon with, friend.

But there was no underground tunnel, and with daylight saving there were a good several hours during which I could clearly be seen if I tried to go home. And—who could say?—with eleven million up for grabs there just *might* be a man lying up on that hill with powerful glasses focused on this house and its every coming and going. I really did have to stay here, and when I finished my drink and the ice rattled back to the bottom of my glass, Janet hopped up with a blinding hostess smile, went to the kitchen, and fixed a couple more.

I think the reason she turned on the record player after a while was just for something to do and maybe to cover up the fact that from the moment the front door shut us in here, we hadn't had much to say. And I guess that's the reason, about midway in the third drink, that I asked her to dance.

I'm going to write a Ph.D thesis on the incredible extraperceptive abilities of what we generally consider our more ordinary members, sensitivity-wise. We expect a lot from our finger tips, but how does it happen that the *forearm,* crossing the small of the back of the girl you are dancing with, can detect to the micromillimeter the marvelous slimness of waist swaying between it and your coat front? How does the tingling palm on her side sense with mathematical accuracy the magnificence of the curve flaring below it? And what of the chest, miraculously alert though buried under T-shirt, cotton shirt, and suit coat? How does it convey its delightful twin sensations, how do the thighs, swathed in pant legs, communicate intelligence of their skirted friends? I wondered, and at the edge of my vision Mother Nature cavorted in double time to the music while doing an obscene strip tease.

Your Honor, ladies and gentlemen of the jury, members of the mob of outraged wives howling under the windows of the courtroom—I couldn't help it.

It wasn't my fault. Somebody pushed me; an evil old lady, I think. The music stopped and so did we. I looked down at Janet cradled in my arms as she smiled up at me, and absolutely apart from my own volition, I leaned down and kissed her.

Oh, my God. No. Oh, *no*. Help. Ahhhhhhhhhhhh! Fifty billion corpuscles raced through my veins, passing and tripping each other on the curves, like the last sixty seconds of a roller derby. From tiny launching pads on the insides of the soles of my feet thousands of little multi-stage rockets rose, slowly at first, then faster and faster up through the entire length of my body, to burst out of the top of my skull like Polaris missiles. Desperate top-priority messages to stop flashed out through my nerve system but were superseded by a far older, more primitive message beat out on jungle drums and signed, *Mother N*. I have the impression that that ever-soaring kiss lasted an hour and forty-five minutes, though it couldn't have because I have sinus trouble and can't breathe through my nose and couldn't have held my breath that long, though I'd have been glad to try, and I'm sure suffocation would have come unnoticed.

Janet drew back, looked up at me, and after grabbing a breath like a man in a swim meet, I was set for another go, old Ma Nature cackling and pounding my back in congratulation. And then—well, I can think of dozens of things Janet might have said or done then, beginning with, "Oh, Sam!" and hurling herself at me again. Or, "Sam! We mustn't! Think of Min!" Or, "At last. How I've waited and longed for this." Or even bursting into tears and running from the room, or slapping my face, or almost anything but what she did. She smiled, very pleasantly, and with incredible yet unmistakable sincerity said, "Thank you, Sam. Thank you very much," and—I don't know how you know these things, but you do. I suddenly knew that against all evidence this newly divorced girl, like many another before her, had lost belief in her own attractiveness and thought I'd done her a sort of gallant favor like asking a fat girl to dance, or kissing the scrub woman's work-worn hand, or some damn thing.

She smiled again, gently, squeezed my upper arm gratefully, and turned and walked out to the kitchen. I heard a frying pan clunk onto the top of the stove, and for a moment I still wasn't sure I'd understood. I thought maybe her mother had told her how to handle men inflamed by drink, and that since she couldn't kick me in the crotch she was going to calm me down with some dinner. But no. I walked out to the kitchen, and while there was a pat of butter melting in the frying pan, some steak beside it, wrapped in wax paper, and Janet had an apron on, there was no least apprehension in her eyes. There was only that goddamned *gratitude*, as she glanced up and smiled at me, and even that was giving way to the abstracted, warning look of a woman busy in the kitchen, who doesn't want you wandering around underfoot. And I knew that to her that kiss was just a friendly, almost neighborly reassurance from her friend's husband, good scout that he was, that she wasn't really so bad after all, and that in time and with luck she, too, might some day have a husband, like Min. Back in the living room I turned off the mental cold shower, reached for the rough towel, and shivering and toweling briskly, finished my drink.

Anyway, the steak was good, and I was hungry.

With it Janet served fried potatoes, and she'd brought home a chocolate cake from Blum's. I had two pieces, wondering if I weren't already beginning to substitute food for sex, the two slices of cake representing Min and Janet, and whether in having the second piece, the very word being significant, I wasn't actually guilty of a kind of chocolate-coated infidelity. Janet prattled away; she was going to tell Min how *good* I'd been to her, she said. All in all, when the second piece of cake was aboard I was glad it was dark and I could sneak home to my wife.

Min met me in the front hall for the home-from-work kiss, full of questions, I could see. But before she could begin asking them she caught a whiff of my boozy breath, turned her face quickly so that my kiss landed on her cheekbone, a maneuver equivalent to a thousand words, and walked back toward the kitchen without a word. Actually, following after her, I was just as glad. I didn't feel I deserved to kiss Min, not yet, and I sure as hell didn't feel like answering questions. In the kitchen Min nodded at the table, saying, "Sit down," and turned to the stove.

There was a plate, knife, fork, cup and saucer, and folded paper napkin on the table. I opened my mouth, held it open thoughtfully, then closed it. That hair-raising kiss at Janet's, followed by my arrival home reeking of booze, had me feeling so guilty that I had the quick irrational notion that to say I'd had dinner at Janet's, after faithful old Min had kept supper warm for hours, would be almost like confessing adultery. I sat down at the table; Min turned from the stove with a saucepan full of canned stew, and like the toothy idiot in the television commercial I began briskly rubbing my palms together, sniffing the air like a bloodhound. For all I know, I may even have said, "*Say,* that smells good!"

Min sat down across the table from me, set her chin on her fists, and watched me force down chunk after gristly chunk of revolting stew while trying to grin happily in spite of the article I kept remembering about how heart attacks generally follow overeating. Finally, her voice cool and yet plainly interested, she said, "Well? What in the world did you *do* over at Janet's all this time?"

I should have been prepared for that, but I wasn't and I shrugged, giving the lie time to project and focus itself on the screen of my mind. I looked at it then. It was a picture of me sitting discreetly, almost primly, in Janet's living room, reading a magazine, sipping a weak drink, and with Janet absolutely nowhere in sight. I converted this to words. "Nothing. Janet fixed me a drink, and I just sat in the living room reading ('Where was Janet?' 'In the bedr—') while Janet fixed supper in the kitchen."

"*Supper?*" Min leaned forward to stare at me, then sat back, shaking her head. "Well, I would certainly have thought that she'd have offered you some! Strange; she must be beside herself with worry. I didn't really expect you to eat here, I was so sure you'd have had supper at Janet's." She nodded at my plate and said, "That was actually for me." I started to speak, but my mouth was full, and before I could say anything, Min said, "Oh, no, that's all right! You go ahead and finish. I can tell you're hungry by the way you've been eating. I'll just open a can of salmon for myself."

No way occurred to me to explain why I was eating two dinners tonight, and with Min sitting there watching every mouthful, I had to finish the stew, with plentiful helpings of hot cholesterol gravy, followed by a large slice of apple pie and a chunk of cheese for dessert, and coffee. When I finished, the sweat stood on my forehead, I was pale and had trouble breathing, and I was waiting for the stab of pain in the chest, wondering if I'd be brave. As I got up to waddle down the hall toward the bedroom, Min called after me, urging me to come back for a second piece of pie and coffee, and in her voice I caught the note, so faint only a husband could detect it, of malice triumphant. As I called back a weak asthmatic refusal, clapping a hand over my mouth, I understood that Min knew damn well I'd had supper at Janet's; and what else she had guessed I just didn't know.

It was early to bed for me, though Min sat up and watched television in the living room. But I didn't sleep well or much. I had what I was certain must be terminal indigestion, and for hours I lay listening to Ruby Keeler tap-dancing in the living room while Dick Powell sang "Shuffle Off to Buffalo." Later, Min cozily asleep beside me, I began thinking night thoughts. About cancer of the colon, radioactivity, *Silent Spring*, Red China, and how the earth was six billion years old and was only a speck of the universe, so what did that make me? About this girl, Miriam Glahn, in eighth grade, who was my partner in the three-legged race at the school picnic, and what she said to me afterward—wow! If I'd only known at the time what it meant. About the seventy-five bucks I'd loaned this guy in college, in my sophomore year, so he could get home for Christmas, and how he never came back to school or answered my letters, the son of a bitch. Could I still collect, if I ever ran across him, or did the Statute of Limitations apply? About Nesfresh. *Mr. Nurdlinger, I'm happy to tell you that I've persuaded Jackie Kennedy to use only Nesfresh for the Easter-egg rolling on the White House lawn.* About sneaking over to Janet's yesterday morning, except that she's awake and waiting, and she calls, and I walk to the doorway of her room, and there she is, sort of half sitting up in bed, in this wonderful nightie, and she says, *Sam, you must be cold! Why don't you just come in here with m—* But I couldn't make it convincing, not with a bellyache.

I dozed off about dawn, and in some inexplicable way—there is much that science has yet to learn—this was a signal to the birds, roosting till the branches sagged in every tree for miles around, to begin chirping like fifty thousand fingernails scraping down a mile-high blackboard, and *Silent Spring* sounded fine to me. Finally they stopped, and I fell into a wonderfully deep, sound, refreshing sleep for seventeen full minutes before the alarm went off.

6

AT breakfast, after I'd had a cup of coffee and was well along in the second (before that point, Min has learned, even though I nod and respond, my mind retains nothing), Min said, "Janet was over a few minutes ago."

Min, I have a confession to make; about Sam and me. "Oh?" I said.

"Yes. She's certain someone is lying hidden up on the hills across the street watching her house through powerful binoculars."

"She's nuts."

"Oh? She said it was *you* who said there probably *was* someone. That that's why you had to stay over there last n—"

"Oh, sure. Last *night*. But they're not going to watch her place forever."

"She says she was up at daybreak watching through the curtains, and she's seen the sun glint on his glasses several times since. They're not giving up all that money so easily."

"Well, what can *I* do? I can't sneak over there now in broad d—"

"We've worked it out, Janet and I. Now don't get mad. Promise you won't get mad."

A headache lurking down among the ganglia recognized this as the moment to strike, and did;

nothing good, I knew, was about to happen. But I was tired, and I didn't get mad or even argue. I walked out to the patio with Min after breakfast, and when Janet came over with her big wicker clothes-basket, I climbed obediently in, knelt down in the posture of a Mohammedan at Mecca, and the ladies covered me with sheets, giggling merrily. Each took a handle, lifted the basket with surprising ease, and carried me over to Janet's as I knelt, jouncing and swaying, head throbbing, trying to see through the wicker slits, and reflecting without bitterness that Somewhere Along the Way I had lost the last of my dignity.

What must the watcher on the hill be thinking? Nothing, the ladies had explained. Men never think about what they see women doing in the way of domestic chores. Scrub a floor six times in one day, and no man would ever wonder why or even notice it. Seeing two women carry a basketful of laundry, no man will ever give it a second or even a first thought. Even if he did, it would simply look as though Janet's washing machine had broken and she'd used Min's. They set the basket down on Janet's patio in full view of the hill across the way. Min left, and Janet picked up the top sheet and clothespinned it to a line. Then, her mouth full of clothespins, she dragged the basket on out of view, lifted off the next sheet, snickered, and told me I could get up now.

I stepped into the house through the open patio doors and for my own numb amusement put my arm straight out before me, in zombie-like sleepwalker pose, and walked right on through the house to the front door. Outside, I got the Thunderbird out of the garage, tapped the horn, and sat waiting in apparent submissiveness. But the truth was that I'd had enough. Janet came out, slamming the door, getting into her coat, straightening her shoulder straps, tugging down her girdle, yanking at her skirt hem, and looking beautiful—all these at once, somehow. And when she got into the car I smiled pleasantly and reached across her to slam her door, studying her knees at close range. But it was more from duty than anything else; actually I'd had enough of looking at, thinking about, being alone with, lusting after, and feeling guilty about Janet. What had it got me but a bad headache and conscience? If only there were one day a year—in the holiday season, appropriately— that wasn't a part of any month and that had no date or even name, and on that One Day, almost removed from time, it was perfectly okay to—

But there was no such day, not yet; society wasn't ready for it, and I wasn't so damn sure I was either. Over at my house a window blind jiggled slightly and I saw Min peek out, and without turning my head I smiled and waggled one finger of the hand on the steering wheel as I backed out of the driveway, and I wished with all my heart that it were the weekend and that I was over there with Minerva, my mate, right now. Tonight, goddamn it, I was coming straight *home*. And after supper I'd mix us a drink, and we'd get to bed early, really early, before we were tired.

About noon Min phoned me at the office. She'd been wondering, too, if there was actually any sense in my being over at Janet's the way I had. Was there really anyone watching the house? Had there ever been? I started to interrupt eagerly, but Min cut me off. About ten o'clock, she said, in the middle of vacuuming the living room, she shut off the machine, got out the car, and drove over to Old Pew Avenue, a shabby, run-down little street planned by the tract designers as our slum area, and which runs along the base of the hill across from us, on the other side. She'd climbed the hill, a considerable accomplishment, and from the top searched our slope with her eyes. I knew what she'd been hoping to find; nothing at all, so that flatly and conclusively there'd be no more reason for my going to Janet's. But Min has a conscience and she had to climb fifty yards down the slope then, to examine a flattened area she'd seen from the hilltop. It was just about the size—she couldn't deny it to herself—that a man hiding to spy on Janet's house would have made. And within it were five cigarette stubs crushed out in the dirt, half a dozen paper matches, and a tight ball of waxed paper about the size you'd wrap a sandwich in. All this was obviously new and fresh, and she also found a nickel lying where it might have slid from a reclining man's pants pocket.

Eleven million dollars, we both suddenly understood, wasn't just a set of words. It was a fortune, a very large one, and someone really had been lying up on the hill watching every coming and going at Janet's. He'd seen me leave and return yesterday, and this morning he'd been watching again. Why? I got irritated; I didn't understand it! If they hadn't been fooled, if they knew I wasn't Janet's husband, then why keep on watching? They already had what they wanted, in that case. And if they didn't know the truth, why should they suspect that the man leaving from and returning to Janet's house each day was anyone but her husband? Was I doing something wrong, something suspicious? I couldn't think of anything.

We kicked it around. Maybe the guy was now gone for good, I said; this morning he'd watched for one last time, in order to be absolutely certain. But I'd come walking out of Janet's house as usual, and now he was convinced and wasn't coming back. Yes, that's true, Min said, wanting to accept it. But she couldn't keep herself from adding, what if he *did* come back? Well, she could go up on the hill again around five o'clock and see, then phone me at the office. Fine, yes, she could do that, all right, except . . . Except what? Well, what if he picked still a third place to spy from? After all, he'd changed hiding places each day so far. He could be in any of a couple of dozen forty-foot pine trees, or lying on a roof hidden from the hilltop by a chimney, or in still another parked car. He might even be comfortably inside one of the two houses across the street, if he wanted to take the chance; no one was at home at either place, their driveways filling with yellowing newspapers and throwaways. We boiled it all down and looked at what was left; tonight after work I had to go back to Janet's.

Somewhere inside me a small boy threw himself on the floor and began kicking his heels in a temper tantrum. *I don't* WANT *to, I want to go* HOME! he shrieked, and in complete sympathy with him I said to Min, "All right, goddam it, I'll go! But listen, the first minute it's dark, I'm coming home, and we'll have supper together. Just the two of us. Get some wine, why don't you? What the hell, get champagne! And while you're at it, don't get that lousy buck-seventy-five stuff; get the good kind, two-thirty-nine a quart. 'L'Okay,' I think it's called. And we'll celebrate. I don't know what, but we'll celebrate." And because Min knew I meant every word, she was as pleased and excited as I was, and when I hung up I was counting on my fingers the hours till I could go home.

I had to walk from the bus stop down Admiral Benbow Boulevard to Janet's house; since all she'd had to do in the city was pick up her new dress, she hadn't stayed all day, so I had no ride home. Studying the hillside across the street from the corner of my eye as I trudged along the last dozen uphill yards in my Homburg and office clothes, a newspaper under my arm, I thought I ought to look suburban enough, husbandly enough, to suit anybody. I sure as hell couldn't look much like anybody's idea of anybody's lover. Looking at my own house just beyond Janet's, feeling low-down and homesick, I wished I could sneak home right now. But there just wasn't any way to do it, and the reason I felt low-down as I turned toward Janet's door was that for the last dozen or so steps I'd been absolutely unable to prevent myself from wondering whether I could get away with kissing Janet good evening.

My mind just wouldn't stop suggesting that if she came walking down the hall to meet me, say, when she heard the front door open, I could stand waiting by the door as I closed it behind me, wearing a look of boyish mischief, and then, in what could only be taken as a sort of lighthearted joke . . .

After the bright sun outside, the hall seemed dark as I came into the house. But sure enough, her high heels came clicking down the hall toward me, and when I closed the door behind me I could see her gloriously feminine silhouette against the light from the other end of the house, and I flipped on the boyish smile and the corpuscles began screeching on the curves. Something about the silhouette puzzled me, and I blinked, saw it was Min, and the boyish mischief flipped over to panic; for an irrational instant I was certain she could see just what I'd been thinking. Then, practically instantaneously, I converted openmouthed panic into speechless delight and stepped forward to kiss her.

It was very nice. In the middle of it, it came to me that it was actually okay to do this. And when I stepped back and smiled down at Min and she saw the look of honest pleasure in my face, she even blushed a little. Then she lifted her face to be kissed again. I was happy to oblige, and in the middle of *this* one it occurred to me to pretend I was married to old Janet back there in the kitchen somewhere, that I'd come home as usual, and was now sneaking a kiss with Min, that splendidly buxom girl who was visiting from next door, and the kiss suddenly turned from excellent to great, and Min thought so, too; I could tell. Then she was pulling away, whispering, "Janet's coming!" and I stepped back in such quick guilty fear that Janet would catch us that I backed into the front door, banging my head, and I wondered if the lobes of my brain might suddenly split open like a giant oyster shell, out of the pitiful confusion I seemed to be living in.

"What're you doing here?" I said to Min, and Janet, who was walking down the hall toward us, answered.

"Our private eye, or whatever you'd call him, doesn't believe us for a moment; he doesn't think you're my husband at all."

"How do you know?" I asked her, and Min answered. Observe this next time you get a chance; women answer for each other all the time, interchangeably, which is hard on the neck muscles because you're always turning in the wrong direction for an answer.

"I was talking to him today," Min said, in answer to my question to Janet. "He actually tried to break in with a skeleton key while Janet was gone. Right in through the front door when no one was watching, but I happened to come around from the side of our house to water the lawn and saw him." The three of us began walking toward the living room at the back of the house, me with my arm around Min, patting her rear, which felt good, and watching Janet's, just ahead, which looked good. Min said, "I called over and said, 'Mrs. Ebbett isn't home!' and that stopped him. He didn't know what to say, and he turned away from the door looking foolish."

In the living room Min and I sat down on the davenport, Janet in a chair across the room. On the coffee table before me were a bowl of ice cubes and liquor, glasses, etc., and I began mixing drinks, listening to Min, who said, "He looked kind of mad at being caught and tried to cover up by asking if I knew where Mrs. Ebbett was, and I said I certainly did, she was in the city shopping. I knew who he was, of course, so I added very pointedly, 'With her husband.' He was still mad, and he said, 'Her husband?' and I said, 'That's right.'" Min suddenly looked over at Janet as though she'd heard a supersonic cue inaudible to male ears, which maybe she did. Because, mysteriously—mysteriously to me, not to Min—Janet then continued Min's story.

"He said, 'Oh, no, he isn't. I don't know who he is, but it isn't her husband, and I'll be back here tonight and fix both their wagons.' "

"He was just furious," Min said. "He left then, got in a car and drove away. Janet wasn't home yet, and I had to go to the store. I just got back and came right over to tell Janet."

"And I don't like it one bit," Janet said. "It's frightening to have some kind of tough private eye sneaking around, spying on me day and night, actually trying to force his way in here. I'm sure he won't hesitate to force his way in tonight!"

The subject now up for discussion—*Should Sam stay here and protect Janet tonight?* and its corollary, *If so, who'll protect Janet from Sam and vice versa?* —was never actually put into words, but we all understood instantly that this was automatically the question now before the assemblage, with Min having the deciding vote. It didn't help to get the meeting off to a friendly start when—I'd just finished mixing the drinks—we all looked down at the table in the same moment, having just realized that there were only two glasses. Then we all looked up at each other, understanding that Janet, not expecting Min, but obviously counting on me, had set out the makings for only a twosome, and that while it was a twosome that did not include Min, it did include enough booze for a fair-sized orgy.

Janet hopped up, heading for the kitchen, and I handed Min one of the drinks, with a debonair Well-this-sort-of-contretemps-can't-be-helped-and-doesn't-

really-matter-between-us-sophisticates smile and shrug.
Min took the glass without a smile, and looked away
coldly to study a picture across the room. I whispered,
"I'd rather have champagne," and she did smile a
little. Janet came rushing back—I had an impression
of her turning the corner at the kitchen door the way
they did in old silent-movie comedies, skidding a little
on the turn, her feet going rapidly for several moments with no forward progress. Then she set a third
glass down on the table, nearly denting the wood, and
snatched up the second drink, and I just sloshed
whisky into the new glass and began gulping it raw.

I didn't say a damn word then, just sat glancing
gravely from one to the other of them, swigging my
booze. Obviously there was only one thing to be done,
but I was going to let someone else put it into words;
no one was later going to be able to say it had been
my idea. Min began by stalling, suggesting that Janet
call the sheriff, but that was only marking time, and
she knew it. A deputy sheriff in the middle of the
night arresting someone, with charges, counter-
charges, and Lord knows what, was the last thing
Janet could afford.

We all sat pretending to think then, but of course
it was plain that unless we simply abandoned Janet in
her trouble, I had to be here when this investigator
showed up tonight, if he did. I doubted that he
would; I thought that probably he'd only been blus-
tering out of irritation and frustration over what he
suspected but didn't seem to know how to prove.
Still, you can't ever be certain of what people will do,
and Janet was worried, and presently she had to put
the question: "Min? Do you mind if Sam stays here

tonight? Just till the detective arrives? I hate to ask. I never dreamed all this would drag on so, but . . ."

I was aware that she'd asked Min, not me, apparently taking my answer for granted; as she could, in that particular moment. Sitting across the room, her lovely brows arched in timid helpless appeal, Janet could have asked me to wade ankle deep, pant legs held up, in molten steel and would have gotten only one answer from me. But Min was made of sterner stuff, and I saw she was close to making the other one.

If last Sunday afternoon the question had suddenly been put to Min—"Is it okay with you if your husband stays with that splendid-looking young divorcee next door? Alone? At night? For an indefinite number of hours?"—the answer would have come popping out before the question was finished. But the camel's nose was under the tent now. I'd already spent most of an evening here; Min could hardly object to that now. And for all anyone could say now, that was as long as I'd be staying tonight. Even if it were longer than just the evening, even if I had to wait till he came sneaking in after lights out, so what? I'd also been here when Janet was in bed, so it was too late to object to *that*. Of course, the big question remained: If he didn't come at all, would I stay on here all night?

That was the one that bothered Min, and it bothered me. I was tired, I hadn't had a decent night's sleep since Friday; all I really wanted to do was to go home with Min, drink the grocery-store champagne, and climb into my very own bed with my very own wife. It had been a kick, all right, sneaking over to

Janet's these last couple days, speculating, wondering, pretending, half hoping. But the part of me that did was only the evil paleolithic remnant left by snaggle-toothed Mother Nature in an otherwise civilized man. It had no real connection with the clean-cut ninety-five per cent of me that was contentedly married to Min, and I was sick of it shambling around—hunch-shouldered, no-necked, shaggy, and low-browed—slobbering over the thought of Janet. I'd had enough of fruitless temptation; I was beginning to feel like a guy standing around with his mouth open for hours wondering whether to bite into a wax apple. At the same time I was afraid of what might happen if you poked old no-neck with a stick; he might just take over young clean-cut. And I was suddenly afraid that Min was about to be a brave "young-married" proving her trust in her husband, and I felt like grabbing her hand and crying, *No, don't leave me! Better not! Take me home quick!*

All this flashed through my mind in the second after Janet's question, like the condemned man's life passing through his mind during the split second between the springing of the trap and the snap of the rope. And I felt proud of the sudden inspiration that occurred to me. Before Min could answer, I set my drink down, smiled reassuringly at this splendid pair—what marvelous book ends they'd make, stripped naked and bronzed!—and said, "Don't worry, Janet. Of course we'll stay," as though she'd asked us both. "If he comes at all, I'm sure it'll be during the evening; otherwise he'd be risking a shot in the head. So we'll stay, and if he arrives, Min is just visiting us from next door. No problem at all."

Everyone was glad to accept that, and we had another drink, all relieved and chattery, then Janet and Min went to the kitchen to fix some supper. I stayed in the living room and had the third drink that gives me the headache and was glad; I felt it was purifying me.

After supper Min and Janet went off down the hall to Janet's room to talk, the way women do without any compunction for those left behind, and I was glad of that, too, and for an equally masochistic reason. For some time I'd had a certain experiment in mind and this seemed a good opportunity for it. I dragged a chair over to Janet's television set, turned the switch, and waited to see what was on. This morbid curiosity derived from the nostalgia I've heard a good many people express lately over what they call the good television programs of five or six years ago. I still watched television then and I'd seen these programs and remembered them. And I'd been working up my courage to answer the obvious question; if they are now remembered as having been good, what in hell can they be broadcasting now?

I found out, turned off the television for another five years, and sat thinking dreamily that if I ever heard nostalgia for what is now on the air, I'd know the mutants had taken over and we were no longer human. Then I surrendered to the events and lack of sleep of the last forty-eight hours and fell asleep or into a coma, and it was twelve thirty-five when Min shook me awake.

If I take a nap in the evening, the wires come down off the poles and lie loosely tangled on the ground. Just barely enough current flows through them to maintain informal communication between my various members and the slumbering brain. I believe that if the current at such times were reduced by even one more watt, I would pass into a permanent state of suspended animation and live for five thousand years like wheat seeds from Tutankhamen's tomb. When Min wakes me up, all I can manage is to lurch down the hall, bumping from wall to wall, shed clothes, and collapse into bed. She shook me now, several times, I began the slow struggle up from the bottom of the well, trying to get to my feet, but Min pushed me back into the chair, speaking directly into my ear, pronouncing slowly and carefully. "No. No, Sam. You stay here in case Janet needs help; we've decided. We've talked it over, and he's probably been watching and hasn't come because I'm here. So I'll go home, and once I leave, I'm sure he'll arrive before long, and you can come home afterward."

I wanted to protest. I felt I ought to, that Min wanted me to, but I just didn't have the strength. Right now a twelve-foot hairy monster could have burst in and carried them both off, one under each arm, kicking and squealing, and it would have been okay with me if he'd just let me go back to sleep. All I wanted was for everybody to just go away, and I blinked, and nodded, and said, "Okay." Min kissed me good night as though I were leaving for the front, and Janet walked to the front door with her and stood waiting in the doorway till Min crossed the lawns and was safe at home. By the time Janet closed the door I was practically asleep again.

But as almost nothing else could have, a sound brought me wide-awake and staring. It was the sound of the lock bolting. That final-sounding *chunk* of a front-door lock at night that shuts out the entire rest of the world had also, it suddenly entered my mind, locked Janet and me in here alone together, and I was instantly wide-awake, the blood stream rippling like a trout run.

7

*J*ANET came walking in to the distant sound of Oriental flutes, her teeth showing in a party-polite smile, and began gathering up filled ash trays as though I'd lunge at her if she weren't busy doing something. She said, "This is wonderful of you and Min, Sam, and I appreciate it."

I stood up, saying, "That's okay; no trouble. Can I help?"

"No, no!" she said, backing away as though I'd begun stalking her around a table. "Min helped me with the dishes, and there's nothing else I have to do but set these down in the kitchen. Min's a wonderful girl, Sam; you're very lucky to have Min."

"Yes, she is," I said heartily. "Min's a dandy kid, all right, Min is," and we both went on like that for what may well have been an hour and a half, invoking Min's name in at least every other sentence in tribute to her bravery and faith and as a sort of talisman protecting us from evil. The result was that we almost instantly became as intensely aware of each other as though Janet had just been cast up on one of those table-sized desert islands you see in cartoons and on which I'd been living alone for a year and a half.

Without pause or punctuation Janet said, "There's simply no telling when he might show up it could be any time at all and there's no use sitting staring at each other for hours you may as well get some sleep in comfort I'll make up one of the guest-room beds for you."

I said, *Don't bother. I'll just crawl in with you, Cutie,* at the same time saying aloud. "That'll be fine. Can I help?" blushing like a fool. Following Janet to the bedroom—*following Janet to the bedroom!*—I began thinking about the Statute of Limitations. The law, in its ancient wisdom, recognizes that the threat of punishment shouldn't hang over a man's head indefinitely. Well, shouldn't there be a Statute of Limitations as to how long a man can be expected to exercise will power? After a certain cruel and unusual length and strength of incessant temptation, the Statute ought to apply, and now if he just broke down and went ahead and did it, he'd be mercifully immune from punishment, blame, recrimination, and all the miserable rest of it. How much are you supposed to *stand?* I thought, following Janet, and I let old Neanderthal out for a moment's air, hunching my shoulders and bending my knees to shamble along after her, slack-jawed and ape arms dangling.

She flicked on the bedroom light and turned, and I quickly stood erect, grinning foolishly. "Excuse me," she said, and—I was standing in the doorway—I flattened myself against the doorjamb to let her pass, like a leprous beggar who mustn't let even the hem of the queen's robe brush his filthy rags. Janet opened a hall linen closet and brought back sheets, pillowcase, and blanket, took off the bedspread, and—each on opposite sides of the bed, wearing fixed smiles, and avoiding each other's eyes—we made up one of the twin beds. *What if I just grabbed your wrist while you're leaning way over the bed like that, Sugarass, so*

*that you lost your balance and fell forward onto the
bed, and*—ahhhhhhhhhhhh, nonononononono, think-
ofsomethingelsequick, two times two is four, four
times four is eight, M,I,S,S,I,S,S,I,P,P,I, put them all
together and they spell Mother Nature, oh, my God,
what am I *doing* here! Janet did the business with the
pillow in the teeth, pulling the pillow slip up over it
like peeling a banana in reverse, and after mutual
expressions of esteem and good will she left, walking
quickly down the hall and into the kitchen, probably
to scour those goddamn ash trays.

I closed my door, took off my shirt, heard Janet's
footsteps come back down the hall, heard them pass
her door, heard her *unmistakably tapping on my
door,* opened it, and was almost hit in the face by a
pair of pajamas Janet tossed in. "You can wear these,"
she said, and was gone, and I turned to look at them;
they'd landed on the bed. They were orange with
black collar, cuffs, and pocket and made out of some
kind of shiny stuff. They looked more like a Halloween costume than pajamas, but they were my size,
and I got into them and went into the guest bath-
room right next door.

I brushed my teeth with my forefinger, using ordinary soap, which actually didn't taste too bad.
Then I stood eye to eye with myself, breathing a little
circle of mist on the mirror and murmuring insults,
striving for originality and aptness of thought. What
a sniveling wretch I was; mentally, the big-time phi-
landerer, physically a poltroon. Look at you, you cur;
mentally unfaithful to Min dozens of times in the last
few days, not to mention other highly imaginative
and beautifully detailed occasions ever since Janet
moved in next door. The one, for example, where

Min is home visiting her mother in Idaho, and Janet twists her ankle out on the patio and calls to you, and you have to go over and carry her in the house, and—that was a good one. How did it go again, exactly? Well, you're out watering the lawn or something, at just about dusk, and you hear this noise and wonder what it was, then Janet calls, and—what the hell, you're over here RIGHT NOW! You're *really over here* alone with Janet, and you're *still* daydreaming, without the simple guts and strength of character to even try to make one of them come true. Look, slob, if you're going to be mentally unfaithful, then why not physically? What's the difference? A hell of a big diff—I mean basically, essentially, fundamentally; you know damn well what I mean!

This suddenly seemed like a promising line of thought; if I were already guilty, I was free to commit the crime. Walking back to my room, I wondered how, exactly, I could go about it? If I were really going to, I mean, not that I'm saying I will, you understand. I turned off the light and got into bed. Suppose I traipsed debonairly down the hall to Janet's room, and she ordered me out? Or yelled for Min? Or just laughed? On the other hand, what if she'd already been trying to suggest, in various subtle ways . . .

I heard the kitchen light snap off. Steps turned into the hall, came all the way down it, I turned, and there she stood in my doorway, magnificently silhouetted against the light from the hall. "Do you have everything you need, Sam?"

I fought back the schoolboy witticism that sprang instantly to mind. "Sure. Everything. Thanks."

"Well. Good night, then." Her voice softened.

"And . . . thank you, Sam. Thanks very much." Her eyes were tender with gratitude, and I had an impulse to get up, take her in my arms, and pat her gently on the back, murmuring, "There, there, little lady."

"That's okay, Jan. Any time," I said cravenly.

She walked down the hall toward her bedroom. I watched her go, then swallowed. I heard Janet's light switch click on, then the slight squeak of a hinge, and realized that Janet was very quietly closing her door. Lying absolutely still, I barely heard the tiny click of the latch. What did that mean? Was she shutting me out? A few minutes later I heard Janet's door slowly open, with the same stealthy quietness, and now my mind was racing. For now, as though I had the sudden ability to read her most secret thoughts, I knew exactly what had happened a few minutes ago, what had happened just now, and what was going to happen next.

From the guilty quietness with which she'd sneaked her door closed, I knew Janet must certainly have thought about locking it, too, afraid not only of me but of herself. Then, in the very act, undoubtedly, of pressing the little stud in the knob that would lock the door, her conscience stopped her. After all, Janet herself had asked me here; to lock her bedroom door as though she were afraid I'd sneak in and ravish her would be insulting. It would be insulting to even *close* her door, as a matter of fact; the night was warm, and she wouldn't normally keep her door shut. To do so when I was here amounted to a definite suggestion that I stay where I belonged. The implication that I might otherwise not was an insult to a friend, so now she was sneaking her door open again. That's what she was telling herself. But of course, *how would I have known her door was locked or even closed?* The very fact that she assumed I *would* know showed that she thought I'd come down there and see. It showed more than that. It showed not only that she assumed I'd come to her room, it also showed—whether she understood modern psychiatry well enough to realize this or not—that she *hoped* I would.

This was the real reason she'd gotten up and opened her door. She hadn't opened it wide, I was sure of that. To do so could only be taken—when I came to her room and saw the door standing wide—as a bold invitation, and out of loyalty to Min she couldn't quite do that. So I knew that what Janet had just done was to get up (probably not even admitting the truth to herself) and leave her door *ajar*—neither insult nor yet invitation, but, and this was the important fact, no rebuff either, an almost Orientally perfect solution.

Listening, hearing the slight creak of Janet's bedsprings as she got comfortable again, it occurred to me that it must now be occurring to her that if I had heard her door close—as I had—but had failed to hear it open—which, of course, I might not have—I would now be aware only of the *rebuff* but not of the subtle invitation that had followed it. Once she, too, had worked this out in her mind, therefore, I could expect her to say something that would let me know —if I *had* heard the door close earlier—that it was no longer closed now. What could she say? Only one thing, really. In the faintly apologetic I-just-can't-get-to-sleep voice that people generally use to say this, she would softly call out in just a few moments, "Sam? Are you asleep?"

I had a diamond-clear vision of Janet lying in a lace-trimmed nightie only a dozen feet away as the crow flies and knew I had to find the right answer. Then it came to me. I'd say, "No, somehow I can't get to sleep." I thought that "somehow" was wonderfully suggestive. "Do you have a cigarette?" And if she said, "Yes, there are some here," it would bring up the marvelously inescapable problem of who would come to whose room. If she brought them here, I could invite her to sit down on the edge of my bed and have one with me. If I went to her room to get them, I'd offer her one, of course, and it would be natural, then, to sit down on the edge . . . Of course the damn cigarettes were probably in that box on the living-room coffee table, and I clasped my hands under my head and lay staring at the ceiling, thinking hard.

I found myself thinking that it might be simpler to just get up and ravish her, and in my mind I heard her screams shiver the silence of the suburban night, heard Min pounding on the back door, yelling, "Now, Sam, you just *stop* that!" I went through all the subsequent steps of my ruin, including a courtroom scene with Min sitting there sobbing, and saw myself, finally, if I were lucky, sitting on a Howard Street curbstone, a skid-row derelict, and suddenly realized that Janet should have called long since. Lifting my head, I heard—well, it wasn't snoring, of course; you couldn't really say that. But it was that deep slow breathing through the nose that is the next thing to it, and I knew that Janet hadn't thought of one damn thing except closing her door while she got ready for bed and then opening it because it was warm. She'd taken no particular trouble to be quiet about it; all she'd actually done was not slam the door or fling it open. Obviously she wasn't the least worried about me or herself, which, when you thought about it, as I did for the next forty minutes, really *was* insulting.

8

*H*OURS later I woke up, knowing in that odd way that you do that it's the very depth of the night, and knowing that again I was hearing a door stealthily opened. There was no question about it this time. But it was the front door at the very end of the hall, just around the corner from my open door, and the tiny sounds awakening me were, first, that of a key very slowly sliding into a lock, its serrations moving the tumblers one by one in a succession of minute clicks; then the key very slowly turned, withdrawing the heavy rectangular brass bolt from its socket. The door handle, squeaking only once, the sound no louder than the breath of a mouse, turned, and the door opened with no sound until its movement was abruptly checked by the bump and rattle of the door chain stretched to its length.

He couldn't get in, and my legs were swinging to the floor. My palms pressed the springs beside me, and as I stood up I released the springs with a quick gradualness that made no sound. Walking on the balls of my feet, I hurried around toward that door in slow-motion speed, feeling my way along the unfamiliar walls, and now I was hearing in reverse the sounds that had brought me awake: the tiny link-by-link clinking of the chain as it sagged, the slow closing of the door, the soft release of the knob, the careful withdrawal of the key. I wasn't scared, I never thought of being scared—I was enraged at the nerve of this son of a bitch. Everything I'd ever read or heard about the complete depravity of the divorce-evidence kind of private detective was obviously true; he was without scruples, morals, or respect for law. He had no human decency, nothing mattered but money, and I just wanted to get my hands on him.

But if he heard even a sound from this side of the door he'd run, and before I could get the chain off he'd be across the lawn and at his car. With his car door locked then, he could start up and be gone. He'd be listening, too, only inches away, and I had to race slowly and without sound. My hand was sliding the chain-end button in its slot as the key was withdrawn from the lock, and the scuff of a shoe sole whispered against flagstone. Then a pebble crushed against concrete, and now the sound came from a window at the side of the house.

I was running silently down the hall in my bare feet, racing him for the side door that opened into the kitchen. The chain was on here, too, but I was here first, and I removed it fast and silently; I wanted this bird to get in. Once again, slowly and with the very minimum of sound, a key slid into a lock. But this was a simple backdoor key and it rattled more, the bolt was looser and noisier, and hearing this ominous sound of someone breaking into a house in the deep of night, it occurred to me for the first time to wonder just how big this guy was.

I might need an advantage, and beside me the tiled drainboard of the sink extended to the wall directly beside the door. I climbed up onto it, and now I stood in a corner of the kitchen, my head nearly touching the ceiling. When the door opened it would bump the edge of the drainboard I stood on and would hide me, and I stood waiting, my heart pounding. If this guy wanted to know whether I was here, not just in the mornings and evenings, but also in the middle of the night in pajamas as I ought to be, he sure as hell was going to find out. I was going to prove it now once and for all—and with a vengeance for three nights of frustration and lost sleep.

The key made its full turn, the knob revolved, and the door opened and began moving slowly through its quarter-circle arc. I stood crouched, knees bent, hands at my chest, fingers curled ready to grab. The door opened as far as it would go, touched the edge of the sink I stood on, and I stared down through the curtains and glass of the door at a silhouette of hat, a blur of face, and a formless black bulk of movement below it. The man looked huge—a midget would have looked enormous now—and I was scared. His head swinging, searching the room before him, but never looking back or up over his shoulder at me, he closed the door part way behind him and took a small soundless step forward. I waited, calves and thighs tensed, till he lifted a foot for the next step, and as he stood momentarily balanced on one leg only, I leaped as though I were diving from a board.

I landed, knees driving into his back, arms grabbing hard around his neck and tightening, and we made the most soul-satisfying, tremendous crash possible. Every window, glass, dish, picture, door, wall, and floor in the house rattled as we crashed onto the floor boards with a sound that could be spelled. *BOOM!* it said, and as the house trembled and rattled, the guy whose head was pressed to my chest, and whose throat was gripped in my locked arms, began to heave and flop like a fish who'd just made a mistake and leaped into the boat. Lying on my side, I was dragged over the linoleum like a cowboy bulldozing a steer, and he made little heaving, choking sounds, and I wasn't letting go while he still had his strength.

Overhead, the kitchen light flashed on like a sudden noon sun at midnight, and I blinked and squinted as I was towed around the floor. It seemed incredible to me at the time, and it still does, that I could actually admire Janet at such a moment. But I could; the picture was permanently burned into my brain. There she stood, mouth open in astonishment, eyes wide and frightened, leaning forward to stare down at us—and reading from top to almost visible bottom, her hair was bound up in a yellow ribbon, she wore a white nightgown tied at the throat with a matching ribbon, sleeves to the elbows, and the hem came to just barely below what are often called "hips." From there on it was just mile after mile of gorgeously long, thrillingly bare, lovely white legs, and though I was being bounced and jounced over the floor, I said, "Wow," and smiled in simple pleasure.

She stared down at us, I stared up at her, he kicked and thrashed and gurgled, and this seemed to go on and on, and I was getting tired. Then Janet screamed —*Ahhhhhhhh!*—and I was vaguely puzzled. If she'd walked in and screamed at first sight of us, I'd have understood. But to stand staring, peering, bending for a better view, and then suddenly scream—that baffled me, and I tried to think as I lay choking the guy to submission. But before I could she screamed again, this time in words. "It's Howie!" she yelled, and I wondered how she knew his name. "Sam, let go!" she yelled now, and began yanking at my arm. "It's my husband!"

9

I DID. I let go, but for a while he couldn't talk and nothing special to say occurred to me. I helped him up off the floor and onto a kitchen chair; he was a brown-haired medium-sized man about thirty years old, wearing a dark suit that was pretty mussed up right now. He was very good-looking. He had the kind of tight wavy hair I always wished I had; his face was lean and handsome and sort of caved-in below the cheekbones in a romantically starved way. You could see why a good-looking kid like Janet had once married him.

I picked up his hat, and Janet took it and stood trying to push it back into shape, while he sat trying to push his throat back into shape, the way you do a squashed loaf of bread. Pretty soon he began testing it for sound, and that was something like opening a faucet after the mains had been shut off for a while. Nothing but short bursts of strangled sound came spitting and popping out at first, then a trickle of rusty speech began, interrupted by little explosions of air and spray. This steadied to a fairly regular flow as he sat cursing, wanting to kill me, but without the strength yet to stand. Then the flow grew stronger and cleared somewhat, though with frequent rusty streaks, the gist of it being who in the living hell was I, and what in the goddamned living hell was I doing here.

I got a little annoyed and stood over him, hands on hips. "*What am I doing here?* Boy, you've got a nerve. You come sneaking in here in the middle of the night while I'm trying to help Janet, and then you want to know—"

"Help her? *Help* her? How do you spell that? I'll *bet* you've been helping her! You *look* like you been helping her! You in pajamas, her in a nightgown that—"

"What do you *mean!*" Janet said, her chin snapping up, her eyes flashing like a lighter out of fluid. "What an absolutely *despicable* remark! How *dare* you!" She looked wonderful, drawn to her full height so that the hem of her nightie crept up another glorious inch, her shoulders back, her chest outthrust in quivering indignation. "Apologize! This very *instant!*"

He slumped back in his chair, arms dangling at the sides. Looking from one to the other of us, stunned, he muttered, "Apologize?" Then he got mad again. "*Apologize?* I come in and find my wife in a nightgown one inch wider than a cummerbund, alone in the middle of the night with some ape in fluorescent pajamas, and it's *me* who's supposed to apologize!" He shook his head. "By God, that's the history of our marriage!"

"We're *not* married, and I'll *tell* you what the history of our marriage was! Once again you demonstrate your truly *remarkable* ability to *inevitably*, each and *every* time, phrase things in such a cleverly *twisted* and dis*torted* way that it puts *me* in the wrong!"

"*Phrase* things?" His jaw dropped open. "God-damn it, it isn't a matter of *phrasing!* It *is* in the middle of the night! You *are* in your nightgown! If you can call it that. All alone with this guy in his moronic trick-or-treat pajam—"

"Of *course* I'm in my nightie in the middle of the night! What else? An *over*coat?"

I opened the refrigerator. There was a bunch of grapes, and I ate a couple. Then I saw a chicken leg on a saucer, picked it up, closed the door, and stood leaning back against the sink, working on the leg, listening and watching Janet; yow! Apparently I'd missed something Howie had just said, because Janet yelled, "I'm not *with* him, as you so cleverly put it! I'm not *with* him at all. He's the man from next door, and he's just visiting!"

"*Visiting?*" He slapped his forehead. "In pajamas? At this time of night?"

"I don't mean now, silly. We were finished visiting long ago and were sound asleep. I mean earlier this evening. And his *wife* was along, if you want to know!"

"Oh, my God. And where is she now?"

"Home, of course! It got late, and she was tired, so she left."

"Of course. But he *wasn't* tired, so he st—"

"As for the pajamas, naturally he didn't *arrive* in them."

"Naturally. Though at this point it wouldn't have surpris—"

"Because of *you,* he had to stay here with me, so I gave him some old pajamas of yours that you never—"

"Why, goddamn it, they *are* mine." He was leaning forward to stare over at me. "Those are the pajamas you bought me the weekend we drove to Carmel! Our second honeymoon, you kept calling it. Now you give them to this gigolo!"

"Oh, don't try to go all sentimental over a pair of pajamas that you flatly refused to wear at the time, if you'll recall! Anyway, what are you doing here anyway? Sneaking around today! Breaking in tonight!"

"I came here this morning to talk to you."

"Well, why didn't you?"

"You weren't here! You were out with your bone-gnawing paramour!"

"Why didn't you wait, then?"

"I *would* have, I was *going* to, only that snoop next door seemed to think I was a goddamn burgl—"

"Listen, you." I waggled the chicken leg at him menacingly. "That snoop next door is my *wife!*"

"Oh, boy," Howie muttered to an invisible sympathizer up near the ceiling. "Now it's *his* wife who needs protection from *me!*"

They went on, the two of them. Why was Howie here, and where did he get the keys? From the real-estate agent, where else? He was paying the rent and was entitled to a set of keys. Would he please stop evading the question; why was he h— If she'd just shut *up* for a second, he'd tell her! He was here because he wanted her to call off the divorce; he realized he still loved her, you stupid bitch. Oh, yeah? Then why come busting in here in the middle of the n— Because when that snoop—when the woman next door said Janet was living with her *husband,* he was damn well going to find out what was what! And what the hell *was* what?

What's it to him? Would he please try to remember they were no longer married, and *please* cut out the absolutely nauseating crap about still loving her! All *he* loved, and was positively *drooling* over, was eleven million bucks!

What the hell was she talking about? He knew very well what she was talking about. No, he didn't; yes, he did; no, he didn't; yes, he did! There was a pause for regrouping of forces, and I found some cheese in the refrigerator and offered it around. No one else seemed to want any, and Howie said that if what she meant was that her grandfather had died and left her his money, he knew absolutely nothing about it and was only here because he still loved her, and that was all.

Janet laughed, very cynically, head thrown far back, hands on hips. Then he laughed, even more cynically, head even farther back. What the hell did this free-lunch loader being here in pajamas have to do with her *grandfather?* Janet explained in full, step-by-step, exasperated detail, then raised her arm to full length and pointed at the door. *Out! Right now!* Listen, damn it; he wasn't leaving his own house in the middle of the night with his wife in—

If he went into that nightgown-pajamas routine *once more,* she'd *scream,* she really would! What's more, she *wasn't* his wife, please get *that* through his thick head! They'd been divorced and would stay that way; now, get out! Not on her tintype; if she thought for one moment—

Janet swung to me. "Sam, throw him out!"

Howie stood up, slowly rubbing his palms together and grinning evilly. "Yeah, throw me out, Pajamas.

Now that I've got my strength back, and you can't jump me from behind, come on. Throw me out!"

He was about my size, but while he was mad, I wasn't. I didn't like this handsome jerk, sneaking around after his divorced wife's money, but that was between them. I just gave him a cynical look and turned back to Janet. "Look, I'm going home."

"Sam, you can't. It would be foolish. You'd only have to come back in an hour." I opened my mouth to argue, but she walked over to me, and stood close, in that damn nightie. "Please, Sam. The detective was watching from the hill yesterday morning. He'll probably be back this morning, too." She stepped an inch closer, breathing on me deliciously, saying, "Please stay, Sam. Please?" and my head nodded itself.

Howie stayed, too. If Janet insisted he leave, he'd blow the whole plot wide apart, he said. So presently, in total silence and with our backs to each other, Howie and I lay in the twin guest-room beds trying to compose ourselves for sleep for the pitiful remainder of the night. He managed pretty quickly, but I lay there beginning to feel sore and bruised, hoping he'd wake up in the morning feeling worse. That wasn't what kept me awake, though, staring up into the dark; it was the thought of what might have been, compared to what was.

Finally I fell asleep, and he immediately shook me awake. I lay gauging my strength, wondering whether there was enough to kill him, but I knew there wasn't just now and said, "Yes?"

He whispered, "Listen, I've got to go to work in the morning!"

"I'm terribly sorry. But at least you can retire at sixty-five on Social Sec—"

"Look, stupid, we can't both leave for work in the morning from here. Janet's supposed to be married, not a polygamist."

"Actually, 'polygamist' is a general term. Specifically, she'd be a polyandrist."

"What?" he whispered.

"A polyandrist. You sound like some illiterate disc jockey. A woman with more than one husband is a polyandr—"

"I don't *give* a damn! I'm telling you we can't both leave from here in the morning, if that guy is still watching!"

"Okay! All right! Fine! But I *have* to leave from here because I'm the guy who left from here yesterday morning and the day before. So where does that leave you?" He didn't answer, so I told him. "It leaves you sitting out on the patio in back of my place waiting for cockcrow. Then it leaves you waiting for sunup and finally for time to leave for work. After which you can walk straight through my house and leave by the front door; I'll phone my wife then and tell her. The guy on the hill will think you live there, that you're just back from a trip, and that's why you weren't around the last couple mornings. Better hop up and get dressed," I said cheerfully, "because you can't leave here after daybreak. You'll find plenty of chairs out on the patio. I trust they won't be overly damp."

There was a silence, then he said grimly, "That's the very best you can suggest, is it? That I wait outdoors?"

"What the hell else did you think I'd suggest?" I said indignantly. "That you wait inside with my wife or something? An absolute stranger? In the middle of the—"

"Okay, okay!" he whispered, and I heard him throw aside the covers, get up, and begin to dress in the dark. "Boy!" he muttered to his invisible friend. "There he lies. In here with *my* wife. In *my* pajamas. And it's *me* who has to get up, get dressed, and get the hell out! Then I wait outdoors because it's *his* wife, of course, that we're all worried about! Hell!" he said to me. "I haven't even got a clean shirt!"

"Tough," I said cheerfully. "Maybe your boss'll notice you're economizing on laundry and give you a raise."

Old Howie got himself dressed, and—I could see him vaguely in the faint light from the bedroom window—he put on his hat, which was never going to be the same after its adventure on the kitchen floor, and draped his tie around his neck. Without a word of farewell, or a single wish for my restful slumber, he tiptoed down the hall. I heard the back door open and shut quietly and lay chuckling to myself with that sense of deep inner peace that a good deed well done always brings. These thoughts changed to visions of Janet only a few steps down the hall in that remarkable nightie. But with Howie sitting out in the dark, perched on the edge of one of those damp cold chairs, it really didn't seem quite right to—anyway, she was sound asleep, obviously, not to have heard us; my entire left side was stiff and sore, and I was too damn tired and comfortable right here anyway.

10

"Wake *up!* Sam, wake *up,*" Janet kept saying, "or you'll be late for work." I opened my eyes and she was standing in the bedroom doorway smiling, wearing a blue-and-white-checked cotton house dress and looking the way other women wish they looked in an evening dress. "Where's Howie?" she said.

I smiled. "Sitting out on my back patio. He'll have to leave for work from my house."

She nodded and walked superbly down the hall as I lay watching, then she called from the kitchen, "No, he isn't. He must be in your house," and I flung the covers back and jumped up briskly; it was time to get up anyway, as I told myself. At the bedroom window I sneaked the drapes just wide enough apart to peek through with one eye. I couldn't see any movement through any of the facing windows of my house. Then a hand across the way touched a kitchen curtain just opposite my window, moved it aside a slow, cautious inch, and Howie's eye stared directly into mine. Then drapes and curtains dropped closed again.

I had a shower, but as I started getting dressed I realized I didn't have any clean linen either. I hate putting on dirty linen, especially socks, and thought about sending Janet over to Min with her teacup.

But that was to risk no breakfast, and I couldn't take that today, so I got dressed.

At breakfast I tried to enjoy the appetizing sight of Janet sitting across the table from me and projecting over it somewhat, but I couldn't. It wasn't that I was in the least worried about Handsome Howie over there with Min or anything as stupid as that. Hell, Min's not some empty-headed high-school kid unable to see beyond the school football hero's vacant good looks. A mature woman, of course, isn't in the least impressed by a merely handsome man; she's a lot more interested, believe me, in what's behind the face, and the *last* thing Min would even *notice,* for God's sake, is what Howie or anyone else for that matter *looked* like. It didn't matter to me in the least that he was over there; I just didn't like the *idea* of it, that's all. Hell, all this guy had done for the last twenty-four hours was make a big nuisance of himself to everybody. Everything was fine before he arrived.

I was running late, so while I got my hat, Janet got the Thunderbird out and had it waiting in the driveway for me; she didn't need it today, she said. As I came walking out Janet's front door, my own front door opened, and—he must have been watching, waiting for me—out came Howie. "Hi, neighbor!" he bellowed. "Driving in today? I'll ride along with you!"

Min came right behind him, screaming, "Goodbye, darling! It's just *wonderful* to have you home again! No more business trips now"—she actually shook a finger at him, smiling roguishly—"for a long, long time!" It was worse than a scene from one of those wonderful deep television dramas of four or five years ago, and while I knew that part of it was for the hillside observer, most of it was for me. I didn't blame her for getting a little of her own back now that the tables were turned, or at least tilted a little. But I didn't have to like it either, and as I passed Janet to get into the car, I patted her ass in friendly farewell, and revenge was sweet.

Neither Howie nor I said a word all the way into the city; we just sat pretending we weren't eying each other suspiciously. Somewhere along Van Ness Avenue I finally said, "Well? Where can I drop you?"

"California and Kearney. Mighty nice of you, even though it's my car."

"Don't mention it," I said, smiling. "Sure you don't want me to drop you at a restaurant first; you must be pretty hungry."

"No. Thanks for your thoughtfulness, but I'm pretty full, actually; waffles and scrapple are a lot more than I usually eat for breakfast. But Min was so wonderfully nice about fixing them for me, I really couldn't refuse. I'm sure you understand."

"Sure. 'Min,' eh?"

He shrugged. "She insisted formalities would be absurd under such intimate circumstances. A wonderful girl. A fine, *generous* girl. Once I explained who I was, after she saw me out there on the patio very early this morning, she just couldn't do enough for me. Good-looking girl, too—watch the road! What are you staring at?"

"Why, goddamn it, you're wearing one of my shirts!"

He nodded, smiling. "Also a pair of your shorts and those wonderful French lisle socks of yours. Generous to a fault, that girl! I tell you there's just *nothing* she wouldn't do for me!"

I dropped him in front of the California Indemnity Building, just managing to refrain from slamming into reverse, backing, then shooting forward over him. Then I drove on to work in my sweat-stained linen and stiff socks, with the feeling that body lice had gotten a foothold.

At the office I phoned Min and said "Hi!" very cheerily.

She said, "Oh, hi," and waited.

"Just thought I'd call and say good morning!" I lowered my voice tenderly. "Haven't seen much of you lately."

"That's right. I don't know whether you're convincing anyone else that you're married to Janet, but you're beginning to persuade me."

There are times, and a certain belligerent defiance in the voice is the tip-off, when it is unwise to suggest to a woman that she is being unfair, unreasonable, and illogical. She knows it, she *wants* to be, and screw you, buddy. I just said, "Yeah," paused, and then in a change-of-subject voice, and also sort of chuckling for no reason I was quite sure about, "So you met friend Howie this morning?"

"Yes!" she said with the first enthusiasm of the conversation. "My, he's handsome! I don't understand why Janet . . ."

I waited, but she didn't finish and didn't need to. I said, "Yeah. Too handsome, actually. That's probably why Janet . . . In fact, she's hinted as much a couple of times." What did I mean? "Well, you know what psychiatrists say. These very virile, overly good-looking guys are practically always queer. Latently, anyway, even though they seem—"

I didn't finish because she was laughing too hard.

"Oh, good heavens *no!*" she said. "Not him!" And she began laughing all over again.

I thought about asking what was so funny but decided I didn't want to know. "Well, I'll see you tonight," I said. "And this time for sure!"

"Yeah, okay," she said absently, then laughed again. "Good heavens!" she said, and was still laughing when I said goodbye and hung up.

I got out my important-papers file, spread them around on my desk, and sat staring through them. Pretty soon Pete Van Freiling stuck his head in my door to say that Mr. Nurdlinger had loved the new Nesfresh board, okayed it without change, and the paint crews had started work this morning; wasn't that great, wasn't the new board terrific? I'd forgotten all about the damn board and hadn't even gone back to the art department to look at the miniature, but I said yeah, it had turned out swell, and went back to my papers.

Janet phoned. She'd made the midmorning trip to the top of the hill this time, and in the same nest Min had investigated she found a crumpled candy-bar wrapper, more cigarette stubs, and the tab from a roll of film. Not only was the guy still watching her place, he was taking pictures, probably with a telescopic lens. *Why?* She just couldn't understand it. If he was all that suspicious, he must have some evidence; but then why not use it, why keep up this spying? Maybe he was a scout for *Playboy,* I said, and Janet would be getting an offer soon. Or he might be a particularly stubborn Peeping Tom who'd stay till he got some action, and the only way to get rid of him was to supply it. She laughed merrily at these droll suggestions, and I felt sad. So would I come to her place again tonight after work? It was a question but a perfunctory one, the answer taken for granted, and while my mouth was opening to protest, she went right on without waiting for an answer. Howie had phoned her and flatly insisted on being around as long as I was at her place, so he was going back to my house after work. My mouth opened again, but she rolled on like Juggernaut. She'd just checked with Min who said it was no trouble at all, to send him around, he was wonderful company; and my mouth clamped shut.

"Sure," I said then. "I'll be at your place. Count on it."

"Fine, and could you pick me up a spool of scarlet thread during lunch hour? Ask for number two and a half mercerized cotton." *My God, only two days and we've got all the trappings of domesticity except . . .* "Don't let them give you plain red now; tell them you want scarlet! And you might pick up something for dessert, since you've got the car. Min says while you're at it, get enough for them, too. She's tired today and doesn't feel like going out."

"Certainly! *Dee*-lighted! Bully! Downtown Montgomery Street is just crawling with little places that specialize in thread and dessert; there's one right next to F. I. duPont Company. All the stockbrokers hang out there."

"Fine. Only don't get napoleons! Howie doesn't like them. Or anything chocolate, because he's allergic. He'd like you to pick him up in the car after work, by the way."

At noon I had a quick lunch, in a place without chairs where you stand up at little three-inch ledges around the walls. Down on Market Street, then, I found the thread in only the fourth place I tried. After work I walked over to a bakery on Sutter Street. They said they'd never heard of chocolate napoleons and would need a day's notice to special-order them, so I got some cookies in two separate packages, got the car from the garage, and drove over to pick up Howie.

Driving home, we were urbane and civilized, chuckling at each other's quips, yesterday's hard feelings buried. But they'd been buried alive and in a shallow grave I realized when I sat in the car in Janet's driveway, watching him walk across the lawn toward my front door; *damn,* he was a good-looking son of a bitch. I stalled, fumbling with the car keys, rolling up my window, till he reached the door. It was unlocked. He just turned the knob, stepped in, and I heard Min screech, "Well, HI, there! How are YEW-W tonight! Come on back; I've got drinks ready. Champagne cocktails!" and the door closed.

Walking toward Janet's front door, I was grinding my teeth so hard that little sprays of powdered enamel flew out of the sides of my mouth, and Janet was standing on the stoop just outside her door, arms folded, lips compressed, foot tapping. "Money!" she said to me furiously, glancing at my house, then turning inside. "That's all he's thinking about; it's all he's hanging around for! He absolutely *disgusts* me!" The door closed, we stood staring at each other in mutual rage and then, in simultaneous impulse, we got even. I grabbed her as she grabbed me; we kissed in passionate fury, and—well, not everything works out at Cape Canaveral, either. The rockets went off, all right; it was great, she was a glorious squirming armful, and my hand began sliding up and down the fine slopes of her back, the swings getting longer each time, rash thoughts prickling my brain. But the rockets didn't quite burst out through the top of my head; they began falling off course and curving downward. Because while my mind did its best to concentrate on the flood of remarkable, excited, and even hilarious messages pouring in to headquarters from the lips, the sensitive chest areas, both palms, the thighs—and even one foot, somehow, in an excited but rather garbled message—it couldn't really give them full attention. It was too busy with, *How do you like* THESE *apples, Min, baby? Go ahead; sit around swilling champagne with that phony bastard who probably wears a hair piece. I'm all right, too!*

As Benjamin Franklin probably said, you can't do two things at once, especially one of them, and when we drew apart we both knew there wasn't much point in a second round. Janet mixed us a couple of drinks in the kitchen, but we didn't sit down in the living room with them. She stayed out there, opening the oven and poking into it with a fork, looking abstracted, her drink in hand; I suppose she was feeling guilty toward friend Min. I wandered out to the patio, drink and cigarette in hand, looked over at my place, and was glad to see Howie out on my patio looking over *here.*

It was Act Two of a summer-theater production of *Private Lives;* a positive flurry of urbane saluting with drinks, tapping of cigarettes, and wry, sophisticated little smiles. Howie had a slight edge in urbanity because he had a champagne glass, but I thought I tapped my cigarette a little more debonairly. We strolled about, gazing around, sipping our drinks, flicking cigarette ashes; in another moment I'd have begun thinking in French. But then a rhumba began on the hi-fi in my living room. Howie gave me the urbane salute, shrugged Gallicly, and stepped inside, and if I'd had eleven million dollars I'd have just given it to Janet and gone home. And on the other hand, wild horses couldn't have dragged me.

I turned and walked back into the house, the full plan in my mind from a to f; in the kitchen I'd just turn off the oven, take Janet by the wrist, and either lead or drag her to the nearest cushioned horizontal surface. But in the living room I stopped with one foot in the air; I knew it was the voice of Superstition, but it spoke loud and clear, and I had to listen. It said that if I made a pass at Janet, Howie would make one at Min, and my foot still in the air, I turned and set it down in the direction of the davenport. There, with a cigarette in one hand, I took another from the box on the coffee table, lit it with the table lighter, and sat smoking them alternately till Janet called in that supper was ready.

We ate in the kitchen, and for a time it was a subdued, even somber affair. But it brightened up when we began ripping Howie apart. I certainly didn't want to knock him, I said, and maybe I was wrong, but in my experience you couldn't trust a man who was too good-looking; they're unreliable, too self-centered. Right! said Janet. Talk about *vain*, why, she used to have to fight him to get to the mirror! She went on about that, and I sat like a kid, listening, nodding, occasionally asking her to go back and repeat a good part. Obviously he was greedy, she went on, and I listened some more. He was boorish, and she gave me examples. He was argumentative, and I nodded happily, stirring my coffee, eating a cooky. What's more, she said, and I nodded eagerly, he was oversexed, and I said excuse me, and got up and walked out to the phone in the hall.

"*Min?*" I said, when she answered *"Are you all right?"*

"Of course I'm all right. What do you mean?"

"Well, nothing, actually. It's just that you looked a little pale this morning."

"You weren't here this morning."

Lovingly, longingly, I said, "Look, baby, I miss you. What are you doing?"

"Howie and I are playing cards. He's really a *lot* of fun, Sam."

"What kind of cards?"

"Honeymoon bridge."

"Oh, yeah," I said, chuckling; it occurred to me that I was doing a lot of chuckling lately for no very good reason. "Great game, but it can't compare with four-handed bridge, of course. How about a game? The four of us? It's perfectly okay for neighbors to visit and play a little bridge!"

"Well, I don't know," Min said. "I'll have to see how Howie feels; he had a pretty rough day at the office. Wait a sec." She was gone from the phone, then she came back. "It's okay," she said. "It's all right with Howie. He says come on over."

"Well, gee whiz," I said, "you sure it's all right with Howie? We wouldn't want to tire him."

"No, come on over. For a while."

So we did. Janet had to fix her face and change her dress, and she said I ought to wear a tie and suit coat. I argued a little. I said it was only next door and that we knew them well enough so that I could go in shirt sleeves and no tie. But Janet said I ought to look nice, so I put them on.

Howie met us at my door in shirt sleeves and welcomed us. While he and I shook hands heartily, the two women half kissed and half nuzzled each other's cheeks in the traditional mixture of simulated ardor and genuine concern for the make-up. Howie invited us to sit down—the bridge table was set up in the living room—then went out to the kitchen to fix drinks. This was all necessary for the benefit of the investigator, if he were anywhere he could possibly see us; this was all standard procedure in Treasure Island where drapes are never drawn when you entertain. I glanced interestedly around the room and said to Min, "Nice place you have here." She was dressed up in a pale-blue dress and looked great.

She said, "Yes, it must seem very different since you last saw it," and we all laughed a little louder than we meant to. Howie brought in the drinks, and we cut for partners, standing around the table, and as my hand touched the cards I had the momentary feeling that he and I were actually cutting to see who'd take both women.

I played a lousy game, especially with Min, though she didn't complain. Just before the last hand Howie, who'd been dummy the previous hand, was out in the kitchen, fixing a final nightcap for us all. Janet was shuffling, and I got up and walked out to the kitchen.

He looked up watchfully when I came in; he knew this wasn't just a social call. I said, "Look, old boy, eleven million bucks or eleven billion, you aren't staying here tonight. I am."

He nodded and gestured with his chin toward the house next door. "Exactly the message I've been waiting to give you about Janet's. Now how should we work it? There's a pretty good moon tonight."

"I know," I said. I had it all figured out; if my bridge had been bad, it was because my planning wasn't. Assuming we were still being watched, I said, I'd leave with Janet. I'd go right out to the back patio then, with a lighted cigarette; he'd do the same at my place, and we'd each know where the other was. We'd allow ten minutes for the lights to be out in both houses. Then the guy on the hill, I figured, would leave for the night, too, but we'd give him still another ten minutes to get packed up and be gone. What if he didn't leave? That was a chance we'd just have to take, that's all. But in order to cut even that to a minimum, Howie and I would run across the open space between the houses simultaneously, on signal from me. This would reduce the time when he could possibly see one of us to only a few seconds. While we were at it, we worked out a plan for the morning, too.

Explaining this to the girls, I watched their faces closely. I wanted Min to be glad and Janet to be sorry. But it was hard to tell what they thought; they just nodded and shrugged and then—absolutely inexplicably—looked at each other and laughed. Howie and Min standing in the lighted doorway, Janet and I left in a welter of glad cries, and we crossed the lawns to her place.

There was a moment when Janet locked her front door, the bolt chunking solidly into its slot for the night, when I wondered if there weren't some way to prop a lighted cigarette out on the patio, maybe wedged into the cast-iron legs of one of the chairs out there so that it faced—the Germans have an interesting legend about what they call *Doppelgangers;* literally, *doublegoers.* Under certain circumstances, that is, a precise physical duplicate of a man is evoked, each one capable of being busy in separate places so that . . . There was a cigarette over on my patio, all right, and after watching it closely I saw it move, and I sat down in a sling chair and looked up at the sky.

There was a high three-quarter moon which gave some light, though not a lot. It was hard to say whether a man across the street on the hillside could see any movement here or not. I didn't think it mattered; if it was photographs he wanted, he could hardly take them now, and I was sure he was gone long since. I could see my watch, and when twenty minutes had passed, the lights in both houses out long ago, I stood up and quietly crushed out my second cigarette. The one across the way disappeared, too, and I gave the tiny little one-note whistle Howie and I had agreed on as our get-ready signal. It meant we were each to stand, still out of sight of the hillside, ready to run on the next signal. We'd considered the possibility of actually bumping into each other, so as agreed, I stood crouched almost directly beside the house, ready to run along the inner edges of the two patios. Howie would take the outer edges, well clear of me. I gave the double-note signal and began sprinting hard toward my house and heard a fearful crash-bam-bang, so incredibly loud the hair on my neck stood up even though I'd instantly recognized exactly what it was; Howie had run straight into the god-damned mobile.

11

IN the center of miles of suburban nighttime stillness my patio was now a clattering, clanking oasis of hideous sound, the mustached photo jouncing, the tennis racket flapping, hub caps whirling in the moonlight, and Howie lay tangled like a trapped fly down in the center of the whole insane web. All my life I'd had the idea, like everyone else, that I could think fast in an emergency. Now I proved that, while it was true, I didn't think very well. Nothing occurred to me except to get him out of there, and I grabbed Howie's ankles, began yanking, and—idiotically in a whisper, as though otherwise he could be heard across the street above the wild racket here—Howie said, "Cut it *out,* you idiot. My head's stuck!" And before I could let go he yanked his feet away from me so hard that I was pulled in after him.

At first I thought I had somehow shut the thing off by falling into it, then I heard a mouselike squeak and looked toward the house. In the open patio doors Min stood in her nightgown, holding the end of the extension cord which she'd yanked loose and laughing so helplessly she couldn't get enough breath to make much sound. It was a silent paroxysm—she staggered—the only sound being rapid little whooping-cough-like gasps, and she raised an arm to full length, pointed to us, then collapsed, sprawling into a chair.

It seems to me that Howie and I behaved with a good deal of dignity, considering that we had one hell of a time getting out of the mobile—our clothes kept snagging on things—and that Janet was out on her patio in about the same state as Min. Women, I've noticed, have primitive senses of humor.

When I finally crawled out of the mobile, backward, I just walked on into the house; what anyone over on the hill, or anywhere else, had heard, seen, or thought, I didn't care. And I didn't care what happened to Howie. I learned later that he'd sat out on our patio for an hour, then sneaked on over to Janet's. When Min walked into the bedroom she was still giggling and I felt a little put out, but when I turned to say something and looked at her, I had to laugh, too, and it was a good thing. Whatever restraint had come up between us disappeared as we laughed, and we went to bed friends, and I was glad to be home.

At five twenty-five in the morning, during the last minutes of full darkness, I was back out on the patio, fully dressed, revived and refreshed by over five long hours of sleep, and ready to sprint. I gave a soft, nearly inaudible whistle; Howie replied from Janet's patio, and the moon gone now, we crouched in the pre-dawn darkness like World War I infantrymen on opposite sides—I was the American, he was the German—ready to go over the top. I waited till a star shell died out over the trenches, whistled twice as I beckoned to my men, and Howie and I darted across no-man's land, this time without banging into anything.

We sat out on the patios then, each of us occasionally and considerately scuffing a shoe to let the other know he was still here. At five forty-five, the sky lightening, the daily New Year's Eve of Birdland began, and I sat coating over with dew, one and a half degrees warmer than a corpse, only the thought of Howie's equal suffering keeping me alive. At six-ten the sun showed, and at six-fifteen we each tiptoed through the other's silent house and came out the front door.

I got out the Thunderbird and off we drove, two neighbors, each with some reason, apparently, for going to his office early today. We were cold, hungry, exhausted, but our wives were inviolate and we even managed to smile when I stopped in front of the big Foster's cafeteria on Van Ness. At breakfast Howie told me—I don't think he'd meant to, but he did—that when he finally got to Janet's last night her bedroom door was locked, there was a blanket on the davenport but no pillow, and he'd had to sleep in the same prenatal two-cushion style that I had at Janet's. I was so glad that not only Min but Janet, too, had been kept safe from this sex fiend that I walked into Burke & Hare with the young-executive spring in my step.

There I had a blow; a new BELS radio commercial was to be recorded tonight. Every BELS commercial had to have bells of some sort in it. This was our own idea; it's how we took the account away from another agency, and now we were stuck with it. We'd already used hand bells ("Hear ye, hear ye! BELS banish belly blues!"), doorbells ("Yes, who's there? BELS for indigestion, ma'am!"), fire bells with the crackle of flames ("Quick! Put out acid burn with BELS!"), a troupe of Swiss bell ringers with a yodeler ("BELSeeeeyelleeyohoo!"), and last Christmas we'd used sleigh bells in the background as a choir sang, to "Jingle Bells" ("Acid burn, acid burn, can spoil your holiday! So get yourself a roll of BELS, and burp those pains away!"). For this newest commercial I'd finally thought of using cathedral bells. We'd persuaded the client it would give the product a certain dignity it may have been lacking, and I'd worked out a new jingle to the tune of "Ave Maria." We'd arranged to record it in the belfry of a local cathedral, but now, sitting at my desk after I'd hung up my hat and phoned Comet for coffee, I read a note from Mr. Burke's secretary, Rose-Marie. The man who played the carillon was a cable-car gripman and couldn't be there in the daytime. We'd have to record this evening; could I be present, please? No answer was expected to this. I had never once performed any useful function at any recording session, but the writer was expected to attend, and I phoned Min to tell her I'd be working this evening.

There is no overtime paid in an advertising agency. It is tacitly understood that none of us works at B&H merely for money; we are there because we are dedicated to the holy cause of increasing the sales of things like BELS and would no more think of asking to be paid for overtime work than a member of the Crusades. So to partially make up for the no-pay evening ahead, I got out my important-papers file an hour or so after lunch and went to visit the art department, which is usually good for a pleasant half hour.

The big room was so quiet, everyone hunched so intently over his drawing board, that I knew it couldn't be agency work. During lunch hour someone had bought a package of toy balloons of assorted sizes, colors, and shapes, and now each man was painting a balloon with whatever suggested itself to his creative artistry: a comic face, a dirty word, an obscene suggestion, a clever enhancement of an original resemblance to some object found in nature. Bert Bishop was painting the tips of a pair of pinkish balloons a rosy red. As a balloon was finished, it was inflated from a tank of compressed air used in airbrush work and thrown out the window to the surprise, pleasure, or occasional annoyance, presently, of pedestrians whom we watched chasing after and picking them up.

After a while I left this pleasant Santa's Workshop atmosphere, and by visiting several other oases, and going out to the cafeteria for afternoon coffee with Rose-Marie, I managed to while away the afternoon. Back at my desk a little after five, I found a phone-call memo from the switchboard; Min had called, and I phoned her back, but the line was busy and I decided to try again later. I was tired of the office, and with a two-hour recording session to face tonight, I wanted to leave now, walk up to Enrico's and have a drink or two, then go get a decent dinner somewhere to brace myself for the evening.

In the lobby I walked out of the elevator, and a man leaning against the wall pushed himself off it and walked toward me. "Hi, there," he said pleasantly, holding his hand out, and we shook hands. "You don't know me, but I sure know you. I'm Reinhold Shiffner, private investigator, and I've been watching you off and on since last Sunday night."

I couldn't believe it. Without ever having consciously thought of it before, I now discovered that my mental image of a detective was a man with a walrus mustache and a derby hat. But this was a clean-cut, narrow-brimmed young executive in a clean-cut young-executive suit and a smile that made you want to adopt him. He could have got a job as an account executive at Burke & Hare on sight; he was Tab Hopper, Rock Rubble, and Rip Snort all in one. "Like to talk to you," he was saying now, steering me toward the lobby doors by an elbow. "And it might be a good idea if we got your car." We were out on the sidewalk now, and he flashed his smile. "A car's the best place to talk; hard to bug, and while it's moving you can't focus the electronic stuff on it." All I did was nod; I didn't know what to say, because it had just occurred to me: who did he think I was, Sam Bissell or Howie Ebbett? My first thought had been: he knows who I really am because he knew where my office was. But on second thought, he might have followed me to this building any day this week, thinking I was Janet's husband. Cleverly I decided to wait and see.

We walked to the garage, and while we stood waiting for them to bring the Thunderbird, I remarked —I had to say something—that he didn't look much like a detective. He smiled; I think he was no longer capable of speaking without smiling; if he'd been drowning he'd have had to smile to yell Help! "I know. Some people think we still wear derby hats. But I'm part of the New Wave: Harvard, 'fifty-five; a science major with a solid foundation in law and business ad. I've got my own lab and fifteen thousand dollars' worth of electronic listening gear. I'll send you a copy of my monograph on 'New Frontiers in Wiretapping,' in this month's *Keyhole*. Some day I hope to have my own jail. As for photographic equipment, you ought to see the beautiful stuff I got with an underwater camera down near Monterey last month; a married skin diver was meeting this girl in an underwater cave, but I nailed him in full corrected color against a magnificent background of sea anemones. Wonderful footage; I'm thinking of entering it in our annual film festival."

"Terrific," I said. "Congratulations."

"Well, thanks," he said modestly, "but there are plenty of us could have done it. We've come a long way, made some important break-throughs. Not much we can't do any more, except read your mind, and that's coming!"

In the car I asked him where to, and he said anywhere, it didn't matter. He'd been following someone all afternoon, on another case, so he didn't have his car; if I felt like running him home, he lived out on Twenty-ninth Street near Geary. I said okay, pulled out of the garage, and turned toward Sutter Street. As I drove, he talked, comfortably slouched in the seat.

He'd been hired by Mrs. Ebbett's cousins, he said, for exactly the reason we'd thought. "I started watching her place Sunday night, from a specially equipped truck I have, and I saw you leave her place for work Monday morning." He shook his head, smiling at my innocence. "But of course that didn't prove a thing to me. In my profession you learn all there is to know about human nature, and I knew that for eleven million bucks she or anyone else would fake a husband if she had to. You could have been anyone, a boy friend, most likely. So Monday evening I came back, this time up on the hill across the street, a better place than the truck. Now, tell me"—he smiled again—"if you even suspected you might be watched, did you really think you could tiptoe through the tulips back and forth between the two houses the way you did and actually fool a professional?"

I just gaped at him, I guess, because he said very gently, "My friend, not only did I know that you sneaked into Subject's house just before dawn Monday morning, and that you sneaked out right after dark Monday evening, but I got a set of infra-red photographs catching you in the very act." We were slowing for a light, and he pulled a slim paper tube from his inside coat pocket, rolled off the rubber band, and opened up two eight-by-ten photographs, holding them so I could see. "Beauties, aren't they?" he said, and they were.

I'd never seen infra-red photographs before, and they were odd-looking; somehow they *looked* as though they'd been taken in darkness, as they had been. But they were wonderfully clear. There I was in the first one, unmistakably, tiptoeing across the lawn in my pajamas, carrying my clothes. Behind me my house was plainly recognizable; so was Janet's just ahead. In the second photograph I was sneaking across the same lawn, but fully dressed and—as the position of the two houses showed—in the opposite direction. He had me cold, no possible room for argument, and I shrugged and admitted it. "All right, you've got me. So now what? What do you want from me?" The light changed, and I started up.

"Yeah, I got you all right, didn't I? It's about as obvious as can be in these photos; anyone could see what's going on, absolutely anyone."

I was irritated; he didn't have to rub in how foolish

we'd been. But he just went on talking, slouched in the seat, rubbing one ear with the rolled-up photographs. "Yep, these are absolute proof," he said, "final and conclusive proof to any private investigator who knows his business, that you really are Mrs. Ebbett's husband."

It took me several seconds to realize what he'd said and a good half a block before I could speak. Then I said very cautiously, "Of course I'm not a professional like you. Just exactly *how* do they prove—what you said?"

He laughed a cynically amused man-of-the-world laugh. "Figure it out. Who the hell else but a wandering husband would sneak over to the hot-looking brunette's next door during the *early* part of the night and then come dragging back home just before dawn, leaving for work a little later like an honest citizen? Lawsee, Mr. Ebbett, I ought to recognize the pattern; I've seen it often enough. Next door there's a widow, a divorcee, or her husband's away. You tell your wife you're going to a poker game; don't wait up, you may be late! Then out you go and sneak through the dark to Mrs. Bissell's, and I don't blame you; wow! Just before dawn you come sneaking home, your pajamas still on, of course, so you can crawl right into bed as though you'd been there for hours! Why, hell, Monday night I reported to Mrs. Ebbett's cousins that the guy at her house just *couldn't* be anyone else but her husband. And that ended the case. I never stretch a job out; it would be unethical."

"I see. And what are you here now for, exactly?"

The smile went on, the mouth opened. "I pride myself on being a creative investigator, Mr. Ebbett.

To reach the top in my profession you've got to have imagination, and naturally it occurred to me that your wife might want photographic proof of your infidelity; with all that dough she'd probably want a new husband and could pay plenty. So I just made my report and said nothing about the pictures. I kept them, and since you seemed to be trotting back and forth every night—I'd seen you come home Monday morning and sneak out again Monday night—I went back to the hill for another set to really wrap this up." He nudged me in the ribs. "But I didn't see you sneak home Tuesday morning; you must have left earlier. Tired, eh? And Tuesday evening Mrs. Bissell was visiting at *your* place. Stayed all evening, and after she left you stayed put. Next morning I saw why; Bissell was home. That night you and the Mrs. played cards over there, and I figured that was that, no more sneaking over there till he goes away again. Sure enough, you and the Mrs. go home, lights go out in both places. I keep the infra-red blinker on steady, but nothing happens, and finally I pack up to leave. The one set of photos will have to do me, and I'm climbing up toward the top of the hill and my car on the other side, when I hear the damnedest noise I ever heard in my life, back of Bissell's place. What was it, by the way?"

"I don't know; garbage can, maybe."

"That was no garbage can, friend, and you know it; sounded like artillery preparation for the Battle of Verdun. Whatever it was, I knew something funny was going on, and I unpacked again, set up the camera, started the blinker, and sure enough—I might have known!—here comes Bissell sneaking over to *your* place." He brought out another picture.

I glanced at it, and there was Howie, one foot up in the air, sneaking over the lawn toward Janet's. "Now I knew what was happening, and just before dawn I proved it." He handed me a long strip of nine or ten small photographs, one after the other almost like a strip of movie film, and I pulled over to the curb and stopped.

"One of the best action strips of my entire career," he said, and I believed him. There we were, Howie and I, perfectly clear. In the first picture we were just appearing from behind the two houses, he at my place, I at Janet's. In the second, third, and fourth we were out in the clear, running across the lawn, every line of our bodies sneaky. In the next two we passed each other; in the following three we were each approaching the other house, and in the last shot we were disappearing behind them. This guy had only been playing with me! Here was the most flagrant proof Janet's cousins could have asked for, an eleven-million-dollar strip of film! "So now I knew how wrong I'd been," young Reinhold was saying. "I would never have thought it was possible, but you damn near fooled me, didn't you? Not quite, though." He reached out and took the strip of pictures from my hand and said, "There's only one thing this could possibly mean."

I've heard Sergeant Friday; I knew a cue when I heard one. "What's that?" I said.

"Wife trading, you rascal!" He nudged me in the ribs. "Good old suburban wife trading, of course; you just can't fool a divorce-case detective!"

12

J ADMITTED it. I shrugged, nodded, grinned, bowed, scraped and tugged at my forelock. He'd done old Harvard proud, I said; he had us cold. He accepted this modestly. While his photos were no good to Janet's cousins, of course, and no use to Janet as divorce evidence since she was so obviously and wholeheartedly involved herself, we were quite plainly hiding these shenanigans from our neighbors. Pictures and negatives were now for sale; ten thousand bucks for the lot. Janet could afford it, he said, and like any other professional man he scaled his prices to the victim's pocketbook.

I agreed. Janet had to buy and destroy these films; she couldn't risk her cousins ever seeing and correctly interpreting them. So I told Reinhold to meet me tomorrow in the same place, down in the lobby of my building, and I'd tell him then when we could raise the money. Don't phone me at the office, I warned him; our switchboard girl invariably listened in.

That settled—we were stopped on Van Ness for a light—I glanced ahead, ready to go when the light changed. Two blocks away, on top of a two-story commercial building on the other side of the street, I saw the most mind-tottering sight of my entire life. If King Kong had suddenly appeared, trotting down the street, eleven stories higher than the tallest building, I couldn't have been more eerily frightened. Because on top of that building ahead stood an enormous already-lighted billboard; a six-foot-high smiling face was painted on it with photographic realism, and—my mind trembled—that giant face was mine. In semi-profile it smiled into another enormous face beside it, which, equally unmistakably, was Janet's, and for the rest of my life I will always understand how a paranoiac feels. For an instant it seemed as though the world had united in a plot against us; staring up at those monstrous faces, I could have believed that they and the truth about us were being simultaneously proclaimed not only from billboards but the front pages of newspapers now appearing on the stands, from television screens, and the cover of *Life* magazine. In the next instant I understood what had happened. Because now I saw that the words painted on that billboard were some nonsense I'd written myself. Running across the top of the board in foot-high capitals was MR. AND MRS. SAM BISSELL SAY, and directly under that, two speech balloons emanated from the mouths of those immense, incredibly familiar faces.

This was no plot: I wasn't paranoiac. The agency and Mr. Nurdlinger, as I'd long since known, had accepted my idea for a candid-camera testimonial billboard for Nesfresh eggs, and as I'd suggested, Art Blatchford had simply snapped someone from the agency to avoid having to get a signed release—he'd snapped me. The clear, sharp photograph enormously reproduced two blocks ahead, I saw, had been taken through the windshield of a car; this very car, in fact. Art had candidly caught me with his Leica, down in front of the building after work on the day of the Nesfresh meeting, sitting in the car with the woman I'd introduced to Mr. Burke as my wife.

The mind is a computer, instantaneously fast on occasion; waiting for the light to change, I glanced up, saw the great billboard ahead, was astounded, baffled, and then understood, all in the beat of a heart. I understood something else equally fast; from the corner of my eye I saw Reinhold beside me turning his head to see what I was staring at. In the next fraction of a second he was going to follow my gaze and see the six-foot heads and giant capital letters which would tell him that the man sitting beside him was not Howard Ebbett but Samuel Bissell—and that the photographs in his pocket were worth eleven million dollars.

I acted. The automatic-transmission indicator needle was already on *Drive*, the motor idling, and I simply jammed down the gas pedal, simultaneously swinging the wheel hard right and turning into the cross street beside us. Reinhold was instantaneously flung off-balance against my shoulder; the great billboard on Van Ness disappeared behind the buildings beside us, and we were driving forty-five miles an hour up the center of a one-way street in the wrong direction.

Six lanes of curb-to-curb rush-hour traffic were parting before us like twin waves at the prow of a speedboat. Brakes howled, tires squealed, rubber burned, horns blared, glass tinkled, metal crunched, voices cursed, others shouted, and we flashed past a man as his front wheels bumped up over a curb, jamming a garbage can under his bumper, sparks flying; his face was red, his fist shook at us, and flecks of foam sprouted from his lips. I got my foot onto the brake pedal, and for the rest of the long block, then, I made our way up the street, zigzagging through the honking, shouting traffic like a salmon fighting his way up Niagara Falls.

At the next corner I swung off onto a cross street, and Reinhold, who was almost completely under the dashboard, began making little sounds—tiny, wordless, questioning murmurs and moans. I felt I understood what he was trying to say and answered him quick-wittedly and brainlessly, making up in speed what it lacked in sense. There *was* no sensible permissible answer to what he wanted to know, come to think of it; if I'd had six months I couldn't have thought of one. Smiling, I said, "Oh, I do that every once in a while. It's good for you; it starts the old adrenalin flowing, counteracting the effects of the soft effete lives so many of us 'moderns' live nowadays." He didn't say anything; he began dragging himself up onto the seat again, keeping his eyes on my face, feeling behind him for the door handle.

I'm not entirely sure he actually meant to open the door; I don't think so. I believe he only meant to press the handle part way down, as a precautionary measure. But I turned into Geary, heading out toward Twenty-ninth Street, and on a brick wall over a used-car lot on the corner just ahead I saw the billboard again—another of the dozen I knew were scattered around town. Janet's and my giant heads behind the fantastically enlarged windshield of this very car seemed to be heading right at us on a collision course, and—Geary's a wide street here—I heaved on the wheel again, left this time, and we began swinging around in a hard, fast U-turn, tires screaming murder, the car trying to lift its left wheels. In the very act of depressing his door handle Reinhold was flung hard against the door. It flew open, and as we turned he hung for two-thirds of his length out of the car in a rigid, perfectly horizontal line, his hand wrapped onto that door handle for dear life, feet braced on the hump that ran down the center of the car. He looked remarkably like the guy making a tight racing turn in a very small sailboat in a heavy wind, hanging far out over the water to counterbalance, and his mouth was wide open and going, "Ahhhhhhhhhh," all through the long moments of that screaming turn, creating a curiously interesting contrapuntal effect with the equally prolonged squeal of the tires.

The moment I could safely take one hand from the wheel—heading straight again, east on Geary now, back toward Van Ness—I leaned over to my right, got a hand on the end of Reinhold's tie, which had a pattern of little footprints, I noticed, and pulled him upright back into the car. "Fooled you that time, didn't I?" I shouted gaily, and jammed down on the accelerator to keep him from jumping out.

I had to get this guy *home* without his seeing a Nesfresh board, and to keep him in the car I drove fast, cornering expertly, chattering wildly. "Sport cars are for *sport,* don't you think?" I yelled at him, swinging to the right off Geary at about forty. "They're fun cars, in the city or on the open road!"

"Why don't you just drop me off anywhere along here?" he said, watching my face and feeling for the door handle. His hand touched it and flew off as though the metal were hot. "Actually I'd enjoy the walk; it's only fifty blocks."

"Nonsense, no trouble at all!" I swung right onto O'Farrell, which parallels Geary, and once again we were speeding west toward Twenty-ninth Street. After twenty-odd blocks Reinhold began to regain some of his color, and I thought it was safe to slow down a little. As far ahead as I could see I kept watch and was beginning to hope we might make it without passing another Nesfresh board. Then I spotted one in a vacant lot, at ground level, and—there'd been a building in the way until now—it was only a block ahead, facing us from across the street. In a moment he couldn't help but recognize those two enormous faces, but we'd already passed the cross street to the right, and at the left along here there were curb-high divider strips down the center of the street; I couldn't U-turn either.

I hit the brakes and Reinhold slid off the front seat. I slammed into reverse, shooting backward, and Reinhold slid back onto the seat after a fashion; I heard his teeth click. Driving in reverse at a good thirty-five, I very nearly reached the intersection we'd passed, when a car came turning out of it onto O'Farrell just behind us. To avoid a rear-end collision I had to jam on the brakes, scorching rubber, then shoot forward fast, and Reinhold bounced like a shuttlecock between seat back and dashboard. There was only one thing to do now, and I did.

Two car lengths ahead a big green municipal bus loaded with strap-hanging rush-hour passengers was trundling along, and I swung right, pressing the gas pedal, and shot up between it and the curb, then hit the brake again to slow to its speed. "Thought I saw a friend back there," I said pleasantly to Reinhold, "but I guess not." We were exactly abreast of the bus, precisely matching its speed, and with the bus running interference like this Reinhold couldn't possibly see the other side of the street. We had less than a block to go—to just the other side of the intersection ahead—and the billboard would be behind us.

But the driver kept glancing over at me, then he began to frown and slow down. I slowed, too; he slowed some more, and so did I. Then he stopped, but I was ready for him; I stopped, too, and he angrily beckoned me to pass. I smiled at him pleasantly and did a before-me-my-dear-Alphonse bow and flip of the upturned palm. He started up again; so did I, and he stopped so suddenly his load of standing passengers swayed like weeds under water. Half standing up, he honked his horn with the heel of his hand, waving me on with a flailing motion; I could see his lips moving. Again I smilingly urged him to go first; he stared at me for a long moment, sat down again, glanced at me once more, then started fast and abruptly, his passengers swaying in the opposite direction. I let him go till the rear of the bus reached us, the bus beginning to cut to the right to reach the bus stop at the corner just ahead, on this side of the intersection. Then, my hand holding the horn down, I shot up toward the front of the bus again, the space between it and the curb narrowing fast. The driver's head turned; he saw me, swung his wheel hard to avoid sideswiping and crushing us against the curb, stalling his motor—and as we flashed on past him and the bus stop, with an inch and a half to spare on each side, I reached over and tipped Reinhold's hat over his eyes. "Did you see that son of a bitch cut in on me?"

I said when he got his hatbrim up and we were past the billboard. "Damn fool doesn't know how to drive!"

I got Reinhold home then, though I had to run two stop lights because I could see he was set to jump out if I'd stopped. The address was a boardinghouse, I saw as we pulled up, which meant he'd undoubtedly eat supper here. I didn't think he'd go out after that; I had the feeling he might go straight to bed. He had his door open as I stopped, hopped out quickly, and stood well away from the car. "Thanks a million," he said, watching me intently. "Do you drive to work every morning?"

"Sure do!"

"Somebody up there is absolutely crazy about you. See you tomorrow at five-thirty, if you're still alive."

13

O_F course all I'd done—I thought about it, driving back downtown—was to postpone the problem. Reinhold might be safe at home for tonight, and I had a hunch that he was, but he was certain to see one of the billboards tomorrow. Near the office I parked, went into a restaurant I go to a lot for lunch, and ordered a drink and some dinner. I sat wondering if I ought to phone Janet; for all I knew she might be able to raise ten thousand dollars tonight, and we could get the photos and destroy them this evening. But of course that wouldn't help either. Reinhold would still see the billboards tomorrow and, knowing the truth then, would be able to testify for the cousins, photographs or not. As for the cousins themselves, what if one of them had been up to the city from the Peninsula today and happened to see one of the boards? There was nothing to do about that except to assume that neither of them had.

Whatever was to be done, and I wasn't sure what that could be, would have to be done tonight; and when I finished dinner I had a brandy and then another brandy to fortify me against the recording session, then walked over to the office and took the elevator up to B&H. The place was dark, but there was still enough daylight to see, and I walked back to the production department. It took me about ten minutes of hunting through their files, careful not to disarrange them, to find what I wanted, a typed list of the twelve Nesfresh billboard locations, which I copied. I had a few minutes to kill before it was time to leave for the recording session, and I walked to my own office, switched on my desk lamp, and sat down, feeling like the guy in the illustration for the "After Hours" column in *Printer's Ink*. You don't actually see him; the photograph they use for the column shows a big New York office building with every window dark except one. But you know that behind that Lighted Window, After Hours, an aggressive young New York adman is Working Late, eager to make first coronary in his age group. I always picture young Ned hunched over his typewriter, staring at the wall of his silent office; with a devotion to his lofty cause, which in another age would have raised him to sainthood, he is thinking up a new campaign. Tonight it seemed to be for cigarettes, always a problem account these days because of those damned doctors, and as I sat idly watching Ned, he began to type, tapping it out with two fingers of each hand.

SCIENTIFIC TESTS PROVE! THE *ONLY*
CIGARETTE THAT PRODUCES
BENIGN TUMORS!

Ned looks at that, sighs regretfully, removes it from the machine, and crumples it. He rolls in a new sheet, thinks some more, then types.

Illustration: Tough Marine sergeant, cigarette
in mouth, leading men Over the Top in
WWI; shells bursting, etc. Headline: *What the*

hell, do you want to live forever? Copy slant:
Be devil-may-care! Say to HELL *with filters,
I'll take a* MAN's *chances and take a* MAN's
cigarette! Psycho connotations: masculinity-
adventure association; makes them ashamed
to worry about health, plus strong implication
that it's un-American.

I began to feel embarrassed, a dirty San Francisco
slacker who had to be pressured into working late.
In New York they obviously *like* to work late, they
enjoy it. It's different in San Francisco; we like to
stop work. Or better yet, don't start. It's the can-
do-but-why-bother city, and *After Hours* is the name
of a bar. At Burke & Hare the only time we hurry is
for the door at five o'clock, the winner generally being
the boss because he sneaks a head start. This is why
New York is so much more successful than we are,
with twelve million people around a bay no larger
than ours, while San Francisco has only a paltry eight
hundred thousand population, and in Marin County,
well within sight of the Top o' the Mark, there are
deer wandering in places a more enterprising people
would long since have covered with tenements. New
York, I salute you! I said to myself. No wonder the
Yankees beat the Giants.

All this time I was aware that still lying on my desk
where I'd left it earlier was the switchboard memo
to phone Min and that the reason I was sitting here
inventing imaginary ads and saluting New York was
to give myself an excuse for pretending I didn't see it.
Still pretending I hadn't noticed it, I asked myself
why I was pretending, why didn't I want to phone
Min? It would be nothing important; she often

phoned me at the office, and I'd been willing enough to try calling her earlier. What had happened since, except seeing Reinhold? What could *that* have to do with suddenly not wanting to talk to Min?

A part of my mind knew the answer, of course, but it wasn't saying just now. I looked down at the memo, admitting it was there now, and I honestly tried to figure out why I knew damn well I wasn't going to phone her and why I felt so guilty about it. Something was up in the murky subconscious, all right, but I didn't know what, and I crumpled the memo, dropped it into the wastebasket, turned off my light, and left for the cathedral.

It was a small cathedral, the larger and better-known ones having been pretty stuffy about our request. This one was south of Market Street, near Skid Row actually, and it belonged to a small down-at-the-spiritual-heels group who needed our contribution. It had once been a brewery, but with the addition of several stained-glass windows made by one of the parishioners, a steeple and carillon, and seats downstairs—after the removal, of course, of some of the original equipment—it not only made a splendid cathedral but easily the best-smelling one I've ever been in. They had the largest Skid Row attendance of any mission in the district, the bishop told me proudly while Max Friedman, our radio and TV man, was setting up his recording equipment in the steeple, and I replied truthfully that I intended to bring my wife here some Sunday. He said they were thinking of emulating various religious orders such as the Benedictine monks, who support themselves by making and selling their own brandy or liqueur, only in this case, of course, they'd make beer, running their batches during the week. I made a mental note to mention this to Mr. Burke, because it might work into a very good account for us with some rather remarkable advertising advantages and tie-ins which other brands just wouldn't have.

Max got set up, and for two hours then, up in the belfry, a girl whose parents had probably sacrificed for years to give her voice training sang about BELS for the belly while the cable-car gripman, still in his uniform, heaved on the ropes. We had trouble with him. In San Francisco a good many cable-car gripmen —he's the man who operates the mechanism that grips and releases the moving cable under the street, the equivalent of a motorman on an ordinary streetcar— exhibit a lot of skill and individuality in the ways in which they clang the bells of their cars; you can recognize certain conductors from the elaborate patterns of their ringing, and there is an annual contest to pick the most skillful. This was one of those conductors—honorable mention in the last contest—and he had a tendency to confuse his two arts. Max worked with him for over two hours, recording cut after cut, but still his tempo wouldn't stay put, and he'd speed up as though he were coming down the Powell Street hill with his brakes slipping. Nor could he quite overcome a certain stridency, together with a peculiar monotone effect, so that at times, instead of inducing a feeling of repose, his rendition of "Ave Maria" had a tendency to make you want to jump out of the way.

All the while, sitting up there, occasionally altering a word or phrase to fit the music a little better, smiling at the thin homely girl singer between cuts, I was aware of a growing sense of depression and irrevocable loss. Suddenly around ten o'clock I understood why.

It came to me, then, that with Reinhold no longer spying on us, there was no further need for me ever to stay at Janet's again. It was a shocking thought. Because it suddenly dawned on me what that meant: that *I was never in my life going to bed with Janet,* and that simply was not an acceptable thought. I mean that I . . . just . . . was . . . not . . . able . . . to ACCEPT it, that's all!

You lob-eared old bitch, there *must* have been a better system; you worked one out for the amoebas, I notice! They just split and go on about their business with no trouble for anyone. But this unwieldy, messy, downright *preposterous* system is calculated sadism, it's beyond the—oh, my God, those long scenic legs, those lovely, bobbling, trembling—now, let's just cut it out; okay? Quit thinking about it! Think about something else. Hear dem bells! Oh, hear de tintinnabulation ob de ringing ob dem BELS. Min, Min, Min, oh, doll baby, you've *got* to understand. I love you. No one else *ever.* You are my dream of paradise completely, sweet Leilani, heavenly flower, so just try to understand now! If I'd never gone over there, as I *had* to, remember, through no fault of my own—alone, at night, with Janet—I could have resisted. Easy! I'd have taken it out in sneaking a look now and then and daydreaming a little when she wore those damn shorts, but not meaning it, you understand, nothing serious, just a little *pastime* like reading the bridge column in the paper or Dr. Alvarez. Matter of fact, even when I *was* over there, I held out pretty well, as long as I didn't know for sure but what I'd be back the next night. But—be fair now! Try to see it from my point of view. Now that I know I'll never again have another crack at—

Min, I don't *want* to be untrue! You know that! And if I'd had any kind of chance at all, if they'd only let me *alone,* I'd have been faithful. I would! But . . .

All right, you bedizened capering harridan, you win. You had to stack the deck to do it, but that doesn't worry *you,* does it? You've been doing it for a million years.

I understood now why I hadn't phoned Min; I'd have had to say I'd seen Reinhold and that now I could stay home, tonight and every night. But I didn't want to tell her and I wasn't going to. No one but me—not Min, Janet, or Howie either—knew the investigator wouldn't be up on the hill tonight. So I was expected at Janet's as usual, until twelve-thirty, when Howie and I would change places on signal. And I was *going* to Janet's, now. I was genuinely help-less. It was out of my control. I *had* to go to bed with Janet just once.

Leaving the cathedral after saying good night to the others, resisting the urge to ask the gripman for a transfer, I knew without thought or planning ex-actly what I was going to do, how and why this one last night with Janet was going to be different from all the others. When Janet and I had both been up and around of an evening over at her place—most of the time fully dressed, besides—we'd each had time to draw back and come to our senses, I told myself. But tonight, when I got back to Treasure Island, it would be after eleven o'clock and Janet would be in bed, the lights out. If they weren't, I'd wait outside till they were. Then I'd go in very, very quietly, and without a sound or turning on a light I'd get into the orange-and-black pajamas that were practically mine now, tiptoe down the hall to Janet's room, and just slip under the covers with her. And Mother Nature, I was certain, would finally have her way. And what was her way was my way now; I was hooked.

"Afterward," as they say, or "later"—well, there was just no point in thinking about that because I had to do what I had to do. Walking to where I'd parked the car, I felt lousy, terrible. But there was no possibility of turning back now, and it occurred to me that in that case there was no sense in letting my conscience spoil the fun. You'll have your day *afterward,* I said to it; do your damnedest then, but *hold off now!* And pretty soon I was able to sort of lock it up, screaming and kicking as I forced the door shut, in a distant corner of my mind and start enjoying the delirious prospect before me. It was a clear night, and driving along the Marina toward the bridge, I could look across the Bay to Marin County, and tonight I could also look across the miles right through the hills and houses, and—oh, *boy*—there she lay in delicious short-nightied, warm-breathed slumber, and pretty soon, within *minutes,* I was *really*—I got a little dizzy and had to slow down on the bridge approach, taking deep breaths.

But up on the bridge, driving over the water toward that agonizing bedful, I was in control, hunched over the wheel like old pictures of Barney Oldfield with his cap on backward, gripping the wheel till my knuckles hurt. Army tanks drawn up in line across the roadway could not have stopped me now; I'd have gone over them. Anita Ekberg seated on the shore of Angel Island—off to my right—playing a harp, wearing a thin white tunic, and beckoning—couldn't have got a second glance from me. I didn't drive fast; off the bridge and on the highway a few cars even passed me, because I was risking no accident, risking nothing stopping me. At a rigid fifty-five, I steered the car around each curve of the road, up Waldo grade and down the other side, on, on, on in the iron grip of relentless lust, and if a highway cop had stopped me for anything I'd have shot it out with him.

I coasted the last twenty yards with the motor and lights off and swung into Janet's driveway, easing to a stop. Getting out of the car and closing the door soundlessly, I didn't dare glance over at my own place. I wouldn't look; I walled it off in my mind. At the door I took off my shoes, slid them into my coat pocket, then took a good two minutes opening and then carefully shutting the door behind me. Undressing in the darkness of the guest room, my hands shook, and if I'd let them, my teeth would have chattered out of strain and soaring excitement. I couldn't find the pajamas in the closet at first and thought about not wearing them at all, but that seemed a little presumptuous, and I found them and got into them.

It was strange, but it was hard to actually start walking down the hall, but I did, in bare feet and without a sound. I was intensely aware every step that, theoretically anyway, I could still turn back, that it was not quite too late. In a minute it would be, in seconds, actually. And at that thought, that within *seconds* I was actually going to be in bed with Janet, my heart started to go till I was genuinely afraid she'd hear it, and my conscience jumped up and began beating on the door with both fists. I think it nearly got out, the door bulging, but it didn't. Because I reached Janet's doorway and stood there, listening to her quiet breathing, and my conscience turned, dropped down onto its cot, and just sat then, face in hands, sunk in apathetic despair. I had passed the point of no return, knew it, stepped forward, took the top edges of blanket and sheet carefully between thumb and forefinger, and drew them slowly back. Very carefully, then, I slid in beside her, hardly touching her—I wanted to wake her gently—and as I felt the wonderful warmth of that glorious body, no possible consequence was too much to pay for what was finally about to happen. Deliciously she stirred, made a tiny sleep-filled questioning murmur down in her throat, and I answered, whispering softly, "It's Sam, don't be frightened, darling; it's me, it's Sam." The incredible reality of what was happening swept through me, and I was suddenly scared, petrified. What if she screamed tremendously at the full high strength of her voice, or fought, scratching and gouging, or shoved at me ferociously?—what an incredible damned *fool* I'd been!

But she didn't. It happened then as I'd wanted it to happen, as I'd imagined it happening over and again. Deep in her throat she made a tiny pleased sound, a luxurious, warm, *sensual* sound, and those lovely arms rose up and met around my neck, pulling me toward the magnificent sleep-warm length of her. I moved toward her, flowed toward her, my arms rising to clasp her to me, saying, "Oh, Janet, Janet, *Janet,* I've wanted this for a long, long time!"

My mind wouldn't work as fast as events then; I had to figure out later what happened. I believe her knees rose up, her feet and arms shoved simultaneously, and I flew—I mean *flew*—straight out from that bed and a yard and a half beyond it, before I dropped down. I landed with a lamp-rattling crash on the floor, absolutely unable to understand what was happening. The bed lamp came on, and she was sitting up, her back to me; then she swung from the lamp to face me, and oh, my God, it was Min.

14

INSTANTLY I understood why she'd phoned me today. Min and Janet had figured out what Howie and I never had, that there was no need for us to sneak through the dark to get to our own wives—if the wives simply changed houses during the day.

She stared at me down on the floor for one, two, three long seconds, her eyes enlarging with amazement and rage. Involuntarily her forefinger uncurled to point at me sitting there—I must have looked as astonished as a human being can look—and she suddenly laughed. She did it helplessly, mouth opening, shoulders shaking, and I began to smile hopefully. Instantly she shook her head violently, clapped her hands over her face, and burst into tears.

I couldn't stand that and scrambled to my feet, and her hands dropped. "Keep away! Don't you *dare* come near me!" she said through clenched teeth. For a moment she stared at me in wonder, in fury, in shock, and—then again, suddenly—in hysterical amusement. "Oh, *boy*, I'll bet you were surprised!" she said, shook helplessly with laughter for a moment or so, then burst into tears again, her head bowing, her shoulders hunching. She darted one last quick painful glance at me, then turned away for good, drawing the sheet up over her shoulder so that I couldn't look at her, and that was more than I could take, and I turned and walked out of the room.

In the guest room I sat down on the edge of the bed, hands clasping between my knees, and stared at the floor. The only thing I knew for sure was that it would be a lot worse than useless to try to speak even a word to Min just now; besides, I didn't know what that word would be. "I was only *kidding*, baby," I muttered experimentally, and tried a light amused laugh. "Naturally I knew it was you all the t—" I shuddered and stopped that. Down the hall I could hear the steady swishing sounds of cloth whirring viciously through the air as Min flung her clothes on. Then she walked swiftly down the hall past my door, fully dressed and carrying her nightgown slung over one shoulder like a limp club, without a glance for me abjectly sitting there. The front door slammed, and I knew the last thing she was worrying about, now or ever again, was a detective spying from across the street.

I didn't seem to have any particular reason to move or even inhale. I tried standing up, but no place to go occurred to me, and I sat down again, though I didn't much want to do that either. I considered getting dressed, but the only place I wanted to go was over to Min, and I knew better than that just now. What I hoped and suspected was that she'd run home crying; that, with Janet comforting her, she was sobbing, laughing, having hysterics, discharging her emotions till she quieted down and could listen to me. *Min, you probably never knew this, but a kind of madness sweeps over men as they near their thirties and the end of the road, and medical science has proved in impartial laboratory tests that they are not responsib— . . . Darling, I had hoped never to have to tell you, but years ago—hunting accident . . . silver plate in my head . . .*

I had to get hold of myself, I knew, and figure out what to really say and do, then I heard a door of the Thunderbird slam in the driveway just outside the window. I scrambled across the bed, swept aside the drapes, and there sat Min in the right-hand seat, a suitcase upended on the floor before her. For an instant I had the confused impression that she was waiting for me to come out, slide in under the wheel, and off we'd go on a trip and sort this little difficulty out; we'd once done just that. But a frayed edge of my mind was nagging at the problem of why, in that case, she'd left our front door standing open. Then Howie came walking out of the house, Min leaned across the seat to open the car door for him, and he swung himself into the driver's seat, pushed his own ignition key into the lock as he slammed his door shut, and I flung myself onto the bed and rolled across it to land on my feet on the other side.

The starter was grinding as I skidded around corners, heading for the front door, then the motor caught. I grabbed the knob, yanked the door open, and the car was backing down the driveway. The rear bumper guards scraped asphalt as the car reached the street, then it swung backward into the road and Min saw me running silently across the lawn as fast as my muscles could pump my legs. Quickly she said something to Howie, and even as he turned to glance at me he was shoving the gear into low, then he jammed the gas down hard and the tires scorched as they shot forward.

I hit the street almost in time—my arm reaching

full length—to touch the car, then I was running down the street after it. "Min!" I yelled, wailed, actually. Then I shouted it angrily, "Min!" But the two red taillights were shrinking fast, saucer-size to cup-size to coin-size. They blinked once as the brakes were touched and they were gone around a curve and the only sounds left were my own panting and the slap of my bare feet against the asphalt.

I ran a few more steps, slowing, then stopped and stood on the silent late-at-night street just inside a fuzz-edged circle of light from a street lamp, staring after those vanished lights, and my teeth were grinding in rage. I was mad—not even angrily, but coldly —and what I was suddenly realizing was simple. I wouldn't have blamed Min for anything at all she might have wanted to do, including leaving me, if she'd done it by herself. But within minutes of what had happened, almost seconds, she was off with Howie. And there was no way at all to make myself believe that could have happened this fast if, consciously or unconsciously, she hadn't had it in mind for some time; if, in a sense, she hadn't simply been waiting for an excuse. Standing there on the street, staring after her, I didn't doubt that Min would never have left me for Howie if I hadn't provided the opportunity. But once I had, she'd sure grabbed it fast, and now I turned to walk home, realizing that maybe Min and I, for far longer than I knew, hadn't been nearly as close as I'd taken for granted. I suppose it isn't reasonable—I know it isn't—but as I walked down Admiral Benbow Boulevard toward my empty house, I felt it was I who'd been betrayed.

Janet was out waiting, pacing the lawns in a blue terrycloth robe, looking anxious, worried, and chilly.

What had happened? she wanted to know. She and Howie had quarreled, but what was wrong with Min? Janet had been in our guest room, Howie in our room, and Min had walked into the house, into our room, and the next thing Janet knew she was packed and they'd left. I didn't feel like talking and just shrugged, said we'd had a fight, and walked on across the lawn and into my own house, closing the door. But my clothes were at Janet's and there were some things Janet had to know right away, so I just walked through the house, turning out lights. When I saw the drawers of Min's dresser standing open, I got mad all over again and slammed the door walking out.

Janet fixed some hot chocolate slugged with brandy, which was very useful, and we sat in her living room —me on the davenport, Janet over in a chair—sipping it. Then Janet laughed. I looked up from my cup—I'd been inhaling the steam to get all the good from it—and she said that the detective across the street on the hill must be beside himself right now. Assuming we'd successfully fooled him so far, he'd just seen Min run out of the wrong house to drive off with the right husband. He'd seen what he would think was Janet's husband run down the street after them in pajamas. Then he'd seen Janet come tearing out of the wrong house and finally see us both disappear into her place. "You know what he'd think was going on?" Janet said, and I looked politely inquiring. "Wife trading!" she said, and I agreed that that's what he'd think, all right, if he'd been out there, but he hadn't been and wouldn't be from now on.

Presently, when I got through explaining all that had happened earlier tonight with Reinhold, the unseeing eye, I tried to tell Janet how important it was to do something about the billboards, but I stopped; she wasn't listening. She was leaning forward, eyes narrowed to study me intently, and the moment I stopped talking she said, "Sam? Why in the world didn't you phone and tell us? If we'd known the detective wouldn't be around any more, Min and I would have stayed in our own houses." She paused, staring at me even more intently. "But instead you came back here, just as usual," she said slowly, spelling it out for herself. "You didn't phone us or return Min's call, so you thought I was still here." She glanced at my pajamas and blushed suddenly, and I took several deep swallows from my empty cup. Janet started to get up, sat down slowly, and then the room was so quiet I could hear an alarm clock ticking far back in the house somewhere.

Several moments passed, then Janet sat back in her chair and murmured, more to herself than to me, "You've gone to an enormous amount of trouble and difficulty. Night after night, and all in my interest. It's been absolutely unselfish, for my benefit entirely. Tonight I think you actually risked killing yourself just to keep that foolish man from seeing those billboards. Now here we sit, the two of us, both deserted. You've lost your wife through this, all because of me." I couldn't think of anything to answer except, *No trouble, don't mention it.* Janet slowly stood up.

"You want to know something, Sam?"

"Yeah."

"After all that has happened, the one thing that would be completely wrong, the one thing that would be truly immoral—is if you still weren't to have me." She'd been undoing her sash; now she wriggled her shoulders and let her robe drop to the floor in a heap around her feet, the way they do in the movies. "Sam, darling," she murmured, "if you still do, then I do, too." And she stood there in that abbreviated nightie in wide-screen VistaVision, a three- and quite possibly four-dimensional daydream come miraculously true. I blinked, but she was still there—even more so —and my knees stood me up and my feet walked me over to her.

What I did then was to stop before her, a sad, gentle smile on my face, and reach out and touch her cheek very lightly with just the tips of my fingers. All the while, out of sheer toughness of moral fiber, I was slowly shaking my head no. Then I thanked her for her courtesy, shook hands, and went home.

No, I didn't. I'll admit that I yielded to massively irresistible temptation. But I didn't enjoy it. My conscience simply would not permit me to enj—

The hell it wouldn't. It didn't say one damned word, not a squeak or murmur of protest. We walked out of that living room hand in hand, pajama legs striding decisively, nightie swaying seductively, and grinning like two kids with a thousand bucks to spend at a carnival. Maybe we shouldn't have felt so good, but we seemed to have the full and benevolent blessings of a lovely, motherly, white-haired old lady I suddenly spotted in the rocking chair over in a corner, knitting and looking at us fondly over the tops of her glasses. "Laws," I thought I heard her murmur as we walked into the hall, "how I love to see the young folks have a good time!"

Hands clasped, arms swinging in happy abandon, we hurried down the hallway, me stealing little side glances and trying to figure how it was possible that Janet, with legs that long, wasn't a foot and a half taller than I was. We turned into the bedroom, flung back the bedspread with the wholesome joy of children on a beach, leaped gleefully into bed, and—Janet began to talk.

It wasn't that I minded a little conversation; I just wanted to postpone it. But she sat there cross-legged, facing me, looking at me with shining eyes, and as women sometimes do at certain times, she began talking about Fate and how it had miraculously brought us together. I thought old Mums Nature deserved at least an assist, but I didn't want to say anything that might prolong the chatter. "Sam, darling, I'll have my final decree in a little while," she was saying then, "and if you went to Reno or Las Vegas, you could get yours at the same time. I could go along, and we could be married right there, if we still wanted to."

This was the first I knew that we'd been considering it, and I said quickly, " 'Fraid I couldn't get away from the office, Jan. Love to, but you know how it is!"

I reached for her, but my arms stopped in mid-air as she smiled fondly and said, "Office? With our money? Darling, you could *buy* the office."

I'd actually forgotten that this creature before me was also *rich*. It was incredible; not only did she have the most spectacular— *Our* money . . . buy the office? . . . *I want you to know, Mr. Burke, that you'll always have a place here at B&H*. My eyes narrowed, and—I wouldn't have thought it was possible —I looked at Janet even more closely. Us? Married? Was it actually possible? What about Min? She might not like it. People do it all the time, though; they divorce the first casual wives of their unthinking youth to marry more sophisticated women who can keep pace with them. Happens every day. Holy cow! All these brand-new goodies, and eleven million bucks besides! Hell of a *nice* girl, too; lots of splendid qualities. Intelligent. Well read. Gorgeous. Rich.

Rich? I said, "My God, Janet—the billboards!" Then I stared at her, she stared at me, and there was a long moment when the bed and the two of us rested on the polished brass pan of an enormous pair of scales, easily outweighing the other one, high in the air above us. Five, six, seven million dollars in baled currency poured onto the other pan and didn't budge us. My arms rose again, so did hers; we leaned toward each other—and eight, nine, ten, *eleven million bucks* dumped onto the scale, shot us up into the air out of that bed and onto the floor, and we landed on our feet and running.

15

WHILE Janet ran to her closet, I tore out, down the hall, out the door, across the lawns—I noticed that the grass was getting thin in places—and into my garage. Babbling to myself that we'd be back by dawn, and that *then!*—I found the old blue jeans, blue work shirt, green baseball cap, and old shoes I generally wear painting around the house, all attractively speckled in a variety of colors, and I put them on right over my pajamas. All the paint supplies I owned were crammed onto a little pine shelf, and I looked at them. There was plenty of white, a dozen unused quarts of it in spray cans, which I bought last spring to do the interior woodwork in a hurry; I'd had to go back to the old-fashioned brush and paint can in an even bigger hurry. I remembered an old fibercloth-covered suitcase out here somewhere and found it. The cloth on one side was ripped and hanging loose, but it still had a handle and the catch worked, and I opened it and set it down on the floor and laid the spray cans of white in it. I tossed in the only two paintbrushes I had, small ones two inches wide, both pretty clean except for the last half inch before the handles. The shelf was crowded with any number of partly filled paint cans in assorted colors, quantities, and states of liquification, and I picked a dozen at random and set them upright on the narrow bottom of the suitcase. I added rags, screwdriver, and hammer, closed the suitcase, and set it in the car trunk.

Janet arrived while I was backing my car, a fifty-nine green Ford sedan, out of the garage. She was wearing black stretch pants, a black turtle-neck jersey, and a scarlet scarf tied under her chin, and if it had been only ten million dollars instead of eleven, I'd have carried her right back into the house. She got in, I backed the car expertly out into the street, gunned it toward the highway, U-turned, bumped back up into the driveway again, hopped out, and stood trying to remember where in the hell I'd left my good clothes this time. I remembered, ran back to Janet's, and found the list of billboards I'd copied down at the office in my wallet in the pocket of the pants lying under the guest-room bed. I gathered up my clothes and out in the car dropped them on the back seat, then sat studying the list under the dome light. The billboards I'd already seen were the farthest west, and I decided to take them first.

O'Farrell Street, way out west of Van Ness, where I'd nearly squashed Reinhold and me between curb and bus, was quiet when we got there; it was after midnight, and the store windows were dark. This was a little neighborhood shopping area, old frame houses on the silent side streets surrounding it. We parked across from the empty lot, turned off the car lights, and sat staring at our two tremendous black-and-white faces smiling across the street at us from the brilliantly lighted billboard. MR. AND MRS. SAM BISSELL SAY ran the legend along the top of the board just above the two heads; in the two speech balloons below it were the words—I winced a little

—of which I was the author. "Give me Nesfresh, I always love 'em and come back for more!" my face was saying in a cloudlike blob of ectoplasm exhaled from my fatuously smiling lips. I remembered what I'd really been thinking, sitting in the car with Janet when that photo was snapped; if *that* had been in the speech balloon, there'd be an overflow crowd staring at the board right now, no matter what time of night it was. Beside my painted likeness Janet's face seemed to be saying, in an excess of colloquialism, "Wowie! Money can't buy better eggs than Nesfresh!" Underneath the two great faces, and running across the bottom of the board, was a reverse panel, white letters on black. This contained the Nesfresh slogan, which had to appear in every ad: ACTUAL HOME TESTS PROVE: *you just can't beat Nesfresh eggs!*

Not a bad board, I thought; those faces reached out and grabbed you by the lapels. "Like it?" I said to Janet, but she shook her head.

"It makes me look older! And my face isn't that thin. And I look much too pale."

"Well, we'll soon have the roses back in your cheeks," I said, and got out, opened the trunk, and then the suitcase.

I couldn't see colors standing back here at the trunk, so I just took out four cans, pried off the lids, and stirred them with a stick from the gutter. Together with a paintbrush I handed two of the cans to Janet, with their lids lightly pressed back on so they wouldn't spill crossing the street. I shoved the other brush and a spray can of white into my back pants pocket and picked up the other two cans, with their lids. Then we crossed the street and stopped on the sidewalk for a look around. But there was no one in sight, no one awake and watching from one of the windows overlooking us in the little apartments above the stores, and we walked into the lot and set our paint cans on the ground before the billboard. There were two things wrong with the board—it bore my name, and our faces were recognizable—and now we went to work to fix that.

MR. AND MRS. SAM BISSELL SAY was too high for Janet to reach. I could just get at it by standing on my toes, and I began to white-out the words. Pressing the nozzle of a can of spray paint, I started at the left, spraying a thick white mist onto each letter. My forearm steadily revolving to keep drops from forming, I worked my way quickly across the entire board, covering the black capital letters evenly and completely, as I could never have done with one coat, using a brush. When I finished and walked out from the board to turn and get a look at what I'd done, the words across its top were gone without trace, the entire background where they'd been a solid white now, like the rest.

Janet, I saw, had painted a pair of wobbly-framed green glasses onto her own black-and-white face; as I watched, she began turning these into sunglasses, painting the lenses solid blue, and with every quick stroke, as the eyes disappeared, the resemblance to herself grew less. I walked back to the board, and working fast but carefully, doing a good job, I began adding a light-brown walrus mustache to my face. As I worked, Janet reached past me, giggling, and added a green mole to the end of my photographed nose. I wiped my brush on the edge of the billboard, dipped it into a can of red enamel, and painted in the tip of a tongue protruding idiotically from

Janet's painted mouth. She laughed, took my brush, and using a Seurat-like technique, stippled my upper lip, chin, and cheeks with red dots, and I grinned at her and said, "Wait'll I get you home," and she giggled. I added some lines to her forehead, joined her eyebrows, heard a sound behind us, turned to look, and a long-haired brown-and-white dog was out in the middle of the lot, trotting along with his head down and his nose to the ground, searching for whatever dogs look for. He was moving briskly in a meandering path, but always drawing closer to the board, his ultimate destination, and I knew what was going to happen, and it did.

As on every night, no doubt, upon nearing the board, he finally glanced up, but now, to his outraged astonishment, he saw us standing motionless and watching him, here in what he and his friends had always considered a community dog park. He didn't stop to consider or search his mind for possible harmless explanations but in the manner of world statesmen instantly assumed the worst and rushed us, barking ferociously in a foghorn bass audible for miles at sea. He was going to bite, I was certain, and I crouched quickly, aimed, and just before he could leap, if that's what he had in mind, I let him have it with the spray can, a short burst of white right on the chops, and he yelped and skidded to a stop.

As Janet and I grabbed up our paint cans, pressing the lids on, he stepped up the volume and frequency of his complaints but kept his distance, swiping at his muzzle with a forepaw. We walked fast, carrying our paint and brushes, and just as we reached the sidewalk a man—he looked familiar—came hurrying along, carrying the dog's leash. He gaped at us, then at his dog, still brushing at his snow-white chops, and I said, "Mad dog! Run for your life!" We ran across the street, giggling, hopped in, and set paint and brushes on the floor mat. As I started the motor, the man across the street was looking at us, up at the billboard, down at his dog, then back at us, making the complete circuit about every three seconds, and I saw—the dog still denouncing us—that lights were coming on in houses along the side street.

I swung the wheel, pulling out into the street, and glanced at the billboard. It was a real spectacular now; two insane, diseased maniacs shouting the superiorities of Nesfresh eggs, and I could only hope that Nurtsy would see it. The man and his mad dog were gaping and barking at us, respectively, from the curb, and as we moved on and left them behind, I realized who he was; I was almost sure of it. It was the bus driver I'd kept from reaching his stop on the corner we were passing right now, and assuming he also recognized me, I'd have given a penny or possibly even fifty dollars for his thoughts right now.

On Geary Street the billboard was painted up on the brick wall of a building directly beside a used-car lot, and for a moment or so I sat stopped in the street, wondering how we could possibly reach it. But then I drove the car into the lot—there were half a dozen used cars in it—and I parked beside the wall directly below the wooden catwalk that ran under the board. When I stood on the car roof, the catwalk was at chest level, and Janet handed up the paint and brushes to me, and I set them on the wooden planks of the walk. I gave Janet a hand up then, from car hood to roof, then boosted her rather pleasantly up to the catwalk. I heaved myself up, took a look around—all seemed well—and again we set to work.

When I'd finished whiting-out the top line, Janet had given herself a pair of extra-large, almost bulging blue eyes; they were crossed and staring at the tip of her nose on which she was now carefully painting a black fly. Brush in hand, I took pause, reflecting, then decided on an Oriental motif, and began the work of slanting my eyes and giving myself a set of scraggly Fu Manchu chin whiskers. From the ground I'd noticed that both above and below the painted billboard area of this three-story wall there was a window, but I hadn't noticed the third window which—both frame and glass being painted solid white—stood in the middle of the billboard itself, a part of the background between the two great heads. Now, as I was finishing the whiskers, I heard the distinctive sound of a window sash being raised, looked quickly around, saw the dark horizontal gap that had suddenly appeared and was still widening between the two painted heads, and I walked over and stooped down before the three-inch-high black slit in the wall just as a double set of finger tips left the bottom of the sash and a pair of eyes appeared to stare out into mine. For two or three, maybe as long as four seconds our eyes stared at each other, then a voice—man's or woman's I never knew—suddenly said, *"Boo!"* and I almost went over backward. This board, I decided, was plenty well enough disguised right now, and we got the hell down off it and out of there, and I wondered, with ten boards still to go, how long it would be before we were arrested.

We had no trouble, though, with the board on

Van Ness. This was the one I'd seen first, on top of a two-story commercial building, and now we parked across the street from it. I wrapped three of the smallest cans of paint in my handkerchief together with a screwdriver to open them and a brush, stuck the spray can in my pocket, and walked to the alley back of the building. I found the fire-escape ladder and, with the four corners of the handkerchief in my teeth, climbed to the roof; Janet waited in the car, ready to tap the horn if she saw any signs of trouble. I had a romantic picture, if the horn should tap, of cops swarming up the ladder after me —MAD ARTIST SLAIN IN ROOFTOP CHASE!—but nothing happened, and in a rather pleasant peace and quiet up there among the vents, chimneys, and rusty guy wires, I gave myself a head of Harpo Marx hair and a black mask, X-ed out Janet's eyes with the comic-strip symbols of sudden unconsciousness, and blacked out two of her teeth.

I thought the cops were going to get us on Bush Street. The board was up on the blank wall of a building at the mouth of an alley, the catwalk under it about seven feet above the pavement, and I parked in the alley at the far end of the board, in the shadows. This billboard faced the sidewalk and street traffic, and while there was no traffic or pedestrian in sight at the moment, we had to be careful. Anyone coming along here could see us standing up there, and we decided that I'd do the painting while Janet stood guard, facing out.

Again we ascended from car hood to roof to the far end of the catwalk, with me boosting Janet, though she didn't really need it, the walk being only a foot higher than the roof of the car. With Janet watching sidewalk and street then, I sprayed out the top line of the board, then pried off the lids of my paint cans. "Someone coming!" Janet said, and we quickly laid face down on the boards.

I heard a man's approaching footsteps, first crossing the street, then he stepped directly up onto the sidewalk, came nearer and nearer, and stopped directly underneath us. I looked down through the spaces between the boards and saw the top and peak of a cop's hat and the silver star and brass buttons down the front of his uniform; I could have reached down and knocked off his hat. He continued to stand there, and I thought he was suspicious, that he was wondering about our car. Then I heard him whistling under his breath and saw that he was rocking back and forth, heel to toe; he was waiting for someone or something and didn't know we were here.

Several minutes or hours passed, I wasn't sure. Then headlights swept across the wall and the cop below us, and a black police car with white doors swung into the alley and stopped underneath us just behind my car. Its lights went out; the door opened on the right side, and the driver said, "Hi, Charlie." Charlie said, "Hi, Lou," got into the car, and the door slammed. By moving my head to the very inner edge of the walk and sighting through a crack, I could see a little way into the car, and the cop who'd just got in was opening a brown paper sack. He pulled out a sandwich, handed the bag to the driver who was out of sight, and they both began eating their lunch and conversing; I could hear the steady murmur of their voices. From their manner—laughing, relaxed—I knew they were here for a while; they probably met every night.

Huckleberry Finn once pointed out that when you wait, motionless and silent so you won't be heard, you begin to itch. It's true. First my knee, then my ankle, then my ribs, neck, head, and arms began to itch, each area expanding until presently their edges met and coalesced into one super and infinite itch, and I had to sit up and scratch if I hanged for it. I did; I sat up and scratched from head to toe, and nothing happened. Their windows closed, the cops just went on with their lunch and conversation. Janet sat up, too, then and began to scratch, and, gallantly, I helped her.

We didn't quite dare to actually stand up and paint, though they wouldn't hear us, but one of them could step out unexpectedly and see us before we could flop down. So we lay there, and time passed, and I got bored. My arm went to sleep, and I let it hang over the edge of the walk. My fingers just brushed the roof of the cop's car, and I thought about suddenly pounding on it, and when they hopped out, denouncing them for wasting time for which I, a taxpayer, was paying, and demanding their badge numbers. The fact is that I don't like cops, not city cops, that is; no good American does. Disagreeable lunkheads, right? And I wanted to get even with them; for what, I didn't know, but I wanted to.

An open can of robin's-egg blue and a brush lay in front of my nose, and I shifted to the edge of the catwalk, my face and one arm over the edge directly above the car roof. I dipped the paint brush in and took thought, but decided—Janet lay at the far end of the walk and couldn't see what I painted—to forego originality and stick to the traditional, only I made the second word *cops* and not *you*. It looked nice when I finished, very neat and carefully done, the letters well spaced and extending nearly the length of the roof. It would be legible, I felt sure, for nine or ten stories up. Still they didn't move, so I went over each letter, converting the entire injunction to a handsome Old English script. No more than half a minute after I finished the car door opened, the foot cop got out, the patrol car backed out into the street, forcing a civilian car to a screeching halt, and rolled off down Bush Street, a splendid sight from this elevation, and one to spark squadroom conversation for days. The foot cop walked off, and within less than fifteen minutes another Nesfresh billboard had been given its unique appeal to all egg-loving maniacs.

16

At the Smiley Hotel I lost my youth. On Sutter Street, east of Van Ness, I parked in the right block for the next location on our list and glanced at Janet in the light from a street lamp. She looked cute, with a smudge of red paint on her nose and several dozen green freckles. I said, "We're not getting anywhere; you're looking more and more like some of the faces we've painted."

She leaned forward to look at herself in the rear-view mirror. "Yeah," she said, and crossed her eyes and stuck the tip of her tongue out of the side of her mouth. "You might as well paint a fly on my nose."

According to the list, the billboard was on the corner ahead, and I looked; there was a five-story building there, and I saw the lighted board up on the roof. It would be somewhat larger, I knew, than a street-level board, in order to be legible from the street. I got out, and with Janet waiting in the car, I walked to the building on the corner a quarter of a block ahead and on the other side of the street. It was old and a little shabby; the brick was stained and the brass plate next to the entrance, reading *Smiley Hotel,* was unpolished. Down the front of the building above the entrance in the middle ran a fire escape; it was the counterweighted kind, the last flight of its stairs suspended horizontally ten feet above the sidewalk. I couldn't reach it by jumping, even with a running start, and didn't dare try anyway, out here at the entrance. I walked around the corner and looked up at the wall there; several windows were lighted, and there was simply no way to climb it. And there was no alley behind the hotel; the rear wall was directly against the building behind it. There just wasn't any way to get to the roof of the Smiley Hotel except up through the inside, and I walked back to the entrance and looked in; a clerk stood behind the desk, reading a newspaper spread out on it.

I knew what to do by the time I crossed the street and walked back to the car. With Janet in the front seat, her eyes modestly averted, I sat in the back and took off my painting clothes, thinking that somehow whenever Janet was around I got undressed. Pulling off my pants, I was momentarily startled to discover I was still wearing the pajamas. I put my good clothes on over them and put on my necktie and hat. I stuffed my painting clothes into the suitcase. Carrying the suitcase with the torn side toward me, I walked back to the hotel and went in.

The lobby was small, dim, with no-color walls, floor, and furniture. There was a staircase and a little open-cage elevator at the right and a blank wall at the left with a large framed photograph of Helen Twelvetrees. Straight ahead stood the clerk at his desk. He looked up as I walked toward him, and I stopped at the desk and set the suitcase down, smiling charmingly. "I'd like a room, please."

He didn't smile back; he was a big guy, two hundred pounds and over six feet, with a jaw cleverly made from one of the legs of a cast-iron black stove.

"You got a reservation?" he said, and I thought he was kidding, but he still wasn't smiling, and I said no. "Full up," he said. "Sorry."

I absolutely had to get into this hotel, and a complete lie instantaneously formed itself in my mind. Since he seemed to be holding rooms for reservations, there must be at least one or two empty for the moment, and I needed one for only a little while. What if I were a salesman, I thought, driving through San Francisco tonight, but my car broke down and was being repaired and would be ready in an hour? In that case I'd be tired, I'd need whatever rest I could get, and might want a room for an hour. I leaned toward him, on the counter, smiling ingratiatingly, and began this idiotic story in a lowered confidential tone. "Well, actually I only want a room for an hour, and—"

Fortunately he interrupted. "Why didn't you say so?" he muttered irritably. "Who sent you—Sam?" Truthfully, I said yes, and he said, "Twenty dollars." I looked at him for a moment or so; how he knew I had to have this room and that he could safely rob me for it was more than I could understand. But he knew, all right, and I swallowed and nodded and pulled out my wallet. There were two tens and three ones, and I gave him the tens. He took them without a word of thanks, shoved them in his pocket, reached under the counter, and handed me a key with a brass tag attached, nodding at the elevator. *Room 434* was stamped on the tag, and I took the key and picked up my bag.

Riding up in the elevator at a good steady clip of five or six feet a minute, I stood watching the clerk gradually foreshorten, saw him reach for the phone, dial, and begin speaking before he was finally cut from view. The call, it suddenly occurred to me, was about me; he was phoning the police or the rest of the gang who for years had been murdering wayfarers in this lonely inn. But I knew that long before I reached the fourth floor they could be here even if they strolled. Anyway, it was a chance I had to take, risks of all sorts, I now understood, being an occupational hazard.

Room 434 was just an anonymous room; a three-quarter bed, a dresser, a wooden rocking chair, a window with the shade drawn. I opened up the suitcase on the floor, took off my good clothes, draping them over the back of the chair, and changed back into my painting clothes. Then I walked to the top floor, found the stair to the roof, and in less than ten minutes, with the speed of experience, I had the top line whited-out and the faces taken care of. It was the best job yet, I felt; enormous handle-bar mustaches with bluebirds perched on their ends, heavy brown bangs coming down over the eyes, and big red tongues hanging out to below the chins. We were not recognizable.

Back in the room, I got quickly out of my shirt, pants, and paint shoes, rolled them up, and stowed them in the suitcase. I had the paint put away, too, all but one can, a paintbrush in my other hand, when a light rapid tapping sounded at the door. I had an instant to wonder if it were Janet, for some reason, when the door opened and a girl—watching the hallway behind her over one shoulder—slipped furtively into the room. Her profile, I saw, was good-looking and she was heavily made up; her hair was silver-blond and she wore red high-heeled slippers and a sort of sleeveless red evening dress. Obviously she'd made a mistake and come into the wrong room, and I was about to say so, hunting for a polite way to phrase it, when—still watching the hall—she closed the door, then turned, took a step or two forward into the room, her head lifting, and saw me. Sure enough, she stopped in mid-step and froze motionless, her mouth slowly opening, her eyes widening in astonishment.

I looked down at myself. In my paint-spattered green baseball cap and orange-and-black pajamas, the fronts of which had also picked up a few paint smears, and with a paint can and brush in my hands, I did indeed look a bit unusual, I realized. I looked up at the girl again and tried to smile in what I meant to be a reassuring manner.

Apparently I failed. She began slowly backing up like a film run in reverse, never taking her eyes off me, and shaking her head steadily. "No," she kept saying. "No."

I didn't know what she meant. "No?" I said. "What do you mean, no?"

She shouted it suddenly, obviously scared. "I mean NO, goddamn it! I thought I'd seen everything, but this is a new one on me!" Her hand found the knob behind her, and she began opening the door without turning or taking her eyes off me, saying, "Buddy boy, you lay a hand or paintbrush on me, and I'll scream the joint down!" She backed out, pulling the door closed after her, then it opened again, she stuck her head back in, and looked me up and down with absolute loathing. "You lousy pervert!" she said. "Just wait'll I tell Frankie!" And she slammed the door.

In one swipe of my arm I grabbed up my good clothes, flung them into the suitcase, clapped it shut, jammed my good hat on over my cap, and headed for the door, a hand reaching for the knob. As I yanked the door open, the girl was just stepping onto the staircase, and she turned quickly and saw me rushing out after her; I figured to pass her on the stairs. She screamed tremendously—my flesh crawled at the brain-numbing sound—scuttled across the hall into the elevator, slammed the wire-mesh door, and nearly pushed the start button straight out through the side. Far below the mechanism clunked, the cage began slowly descending, and as I raced for the staircase the girl in red, her mouth wide open and screaming steadily, was sinking from view like a prima donna in the last act of *Faust*.

We kept a pretty even pace. On the straightaways, taking two and three steps at a time, I'd gain a little, but I generally lost ground on the stair landings and turns, the elevator sinking into view again from the floor above, the volume of that permanent scream rising. Doors were flying open and faces staring out as I rounded the turn on the third floor, and as I hit the second—I think otherwise I'd have won going away handily—my suitcase banged a newel post. I felt the lid burst open and clapped my other hand on it just in time. But for the rest of the way I had to hobble sidewise, one hand on the handle, the other reaching around to hold the bag shut, and the upper half of my good pants, caught in the opening and dragging down the stairs after me, had a tendency to snag on my feet.

In a dramatic photo finish with the most sustained high C since Madame Galli-Curci, I rounded the far turn and into the straightaway, heading for the lobby; Frankie, the two-hundred-pound clerk, stood at the bottom of the stairs waiting for me, arms outspread and fingers curled like a gorilla. But as he saw me appear in my colorful pajamas, baseball cap and Homburg, and coming at him sort of sideways, his mouth opened in surprise, and it occurred to me to growl at him deep in my throat, bare my teeth, and make rapid snapping motions, and after an instant's deep thought he stepped quickly out of the way, and I tore through the lobby, out through the door, and banged into a couple passing by on the sidewalk. It nearly knocked us all over, but I didn't think it was worth while stopping to explain. Staggering into the street, I looked back over my shoulder and made the growling sounds again, snapping my teeth, and the guy decided to let well enough alone. Janet saw me coming—I was hard to miss, hobbling down the middle of Sutter Street—and she started the car motor.

At the car, heaving the suitcase into the back seat, I looked back. Frankie stood outside the hotel doorway staring after me, the girl in red behind him and peering out past his arm. The couple on the sidewalk stood on the curb looking first at me, then back at Frankie and the girl, then at me again. "All right," I yelled down the street at them. "So I'm a day behind in my rent!" And with considerable dignity, I thought, I walked to the driver's seat and got in. I didn't start right up; I stuck an arm out and pointed at the hotel roof, and Frankie frowned, wondering what I meant. But I motioned more vigorously, and he walked out cautiously, with the girl, and—joined by the couple on the sidewalk—they crossed the street, watching me warily. On the walk across from the hotel they turned and looked up at the roof and the brilliantly lighted newly painted billboard, and I drove ahead toward them. As we passed the four of them staring up at that billboard with their mouths open, I let out the wildest, most high-pitched, maniacal laugh I could manage. Janet shot away from me across the seat, and it even frightened me a little, but I felt that the little group on the walk now had a story for their grandchildren on many a wintry night to come.

Eight blocks away, in an alley, I climbed over into the back seat and got into my clothes again.

17

WE drove on then, on our way to the next board as usual, but now something was suddenly different; within blocks the very look of the streets and the feel of the air on our faces had altered. The breeze flowing into the car was cooler and of a different quality, and the streets had become silent and dead. Most people had now been asleep a long time, and the very last events of the day and the night that belonged to it had ended sometime in the minutes just past. All of it had turned into yesterday, but tomorrow hadn't yet begun. It was after three, a time of morning, night, or neither one, when something begins to happen to people who have stayed awake. I was suddenly tired right down into the marrow of my bones, but what happens somewhere between three and four o'clock in the morning, if you haven't been asleep, is also in the mind. You reach a time—we've all experienced this—when things you're normally sure of become uncertain. Were you really once a junior in high school, vice-president of Hi-Y, and is it simply the successive events of each moment ever since that have brought you from there to here? No, there is something else that is pertinent that you know you've missed. Nothing is certain now, and familiar things become strange.

Beside me, Janet had turned back into being a girl I hadn't even known only a short time ago. I told myself that this was *Janet,* that she was about to become rich, that she was beautiful and fearsomely desirable, and that I could marry her, I *really could,* because Min had left me, and from now on everything was going to be changed. But all reality had drained from these thoughts; my stomach felt empty but without hunger, and the work still ahead of us tonight now seemed impossible.

In a commuters' parking lot at the edge of the downtown area we climbed up onto the five-foot-high catwalk of another billboard, but now each move was an effort and boosting Janet was just work. We'd had some narrow escapes, I was superstitiously sure we were about to be arrested, and I told Janet to just keep watch, that I'd do the painting. She agreed with an abrupt little nod, and I realized that if we didn't watch ourselves we could suddenly find ourselves quarreling.

With Janet facing the street, watching and listening, I walked to the left side of the board, shaking up a spray can of white paint. Once again, my forearm steadily revolving, I began whiting-out MR. AND MRS. SAM BISSELL SAY. The spray can hissing as I side-stepped to the right, I spread a smooth thick coat over MR., then AND, and then MRS.

"Car coming," Janet said, and we lay down on the boards, faces on our folded arms. I could have gone to sleep as the car approached, passed, and was gone. But I got up again and stood looking up at the billboard, shaking the spray can, ready to resume. The vanished words I'd painted out had been over Janet's head and speech balloon, running to about the middle of the board. From there on the words still left were over my painted face and balloon, and I looked up at them. SAM BISSELL SAY, they now read Orientally, and I smiled tiredly and looked down at the speech balloon just under them to read once more what Sam Bissell say and had wrote.

> *Give me Nesfresh.*
> *I always love 'em*
> *and come back for more!*

said the foolish words in the cloud attached to my giant likeness, and I was standing there looking at them and shaking my head, but I didn't know why.

Then, out loud but muttering it, speaking to myself, I said, "No. That's not what Sam Bissell say. It's not what he say at all." As always, I'd opened several cans of paint, and they stood at the back of the catwalk up against the billboard, a paintbrush lying beside them. I picked up the brush, dipped it into the black paint, and wiped off the excess on the lip of the can. Carefully, doing a good job, I added an S to the final word of the line over my huge painted face. SAM BISSELL SAYS, it read now, and I stood staring up at it. I didn't know what he was going to say, but I was suddenly and absolutely certain of the first word, and I reached up to that speech balloon and painted it. In letters so big, thick-stroked, and tall that it stuck up over the top edge of the balloon, I painted MIN! I stepped back to stare at it, then at the words just below, and now I knew what Sam Bissell had to say.

In a dozen seconds with the spray can I whited-out *Nesfresh, 'em, and,* and *for more.* Before the first word I painted in *F, o,* and *r;* with three vertical strokes I changed *I* to *I'll;* in the place where *'em* had been I painted in *you.* Then I stepped back to read what I'd done.

From my enormous painted face, just under the line SAM BISSELL SAYS, there now came the words:

> *MIN!*
> *Forgive me*
> *I'll always love*   *you*
> *come back*   *!*

After a moment I began to nod; then, like the great photographed face before which I stood, I grinned with pleasure. I heard a sound and turned to look at Janet; I'd simply forgotten her. She was standing at the edge of the catwalk, staring up at what I'd done. She was nodding, too, and when she turned to meet my eyes, I saw that she was crying. But she was also smiling, her eyes excited and alive, and she said, "Yes. Oh, yes, Sam! Give me that brush." Then she walked over to her own huge likeness and looked up at it, studying the words in the big speech balloon. After a few moments she smiled again, picked up a spray can, and went to work. A few minutes later the words from her billboard mouth said:

> *HOWIE! Money can't buy*
> *what I've lost.*
> *Take me back!*

Standing at the trunk of the car parked at the curb, putting away our paint, we stared across the empty

cinder lot at the billboard. I was no longer tired; I
was electric with energy and for the first time in
quite a long while almost happy. There were our
great lighted faces saying what we wanted to say,
and we looked at them and at what we had done
and admired it. Then I saw one incongruity. Running clear across the bottom of the board it still
said: "ACTUAL HOME TESTS PROVE: you just can't beat
Nesfresh eggs," and I picked up the spray can, black
paint, and brush and walked back across the lot to
the billboard.

Sitting in the car again, ready to drive on, I reread
my message to Min, Janet reread hers to Howie, then
we looked down at the line across the bottom which
summed up now exactly how we felt. "ACTUAL HOME
TESTS PROVE: you just can't beat love and marriage,"
it said in complete truth. Then we drove on; we had
just as many of these boards to paint as we could
possibly get done between now and daylight.

We didn't get to them all. We ran out of paint before dawn, and there was a board out in the Mission
district we didn't do, another near Golden Gate Park,
and one on the freeway to Candlestick Park. But we
did the best we could, and our painted faces shouted
our silent pleas all over the heart of San Francisco.

Then we drove home, parted with flicks of the
hand and tired smiles, and I went into my own house,
got into my own pajamas, and crept into my own
bed. Just before I went to sleep, it occurred to me to
wonder what Mr. Nurdlinger would think when he
saw his billboards. For all I knew, he might like
them; certainly the first ones we'd painted were real
attention-getters. Or they might send him into permanent retreat. I didn't know—I could be fired or

made vice-president—but right now I didn't care which.

It was several hours later when something woke me. I opened my eyes, and Min was standing in the doorway looking at me, her suitcase in her hand. I looked at her, blinking, and got up on one elbow; I didn't know what to say and wasn't too sure why she was back. But she smiled, grimly and very slightly, but a smile. "I saw your ad," she said, "and thought I'd inquire about the position."

I nodded and swallowed. "Well, it's not much, Lord knows. But it's yours if you want it. And it's permanent; no one else qualifies." Min set down her suitcase, walked over, sat on the edge of the bed, and then I had a lot to say. "Min, listen," I began, but she shook her head.

"No, Sam. I don't want to hear—ever—even a word about what happened. No explanations, excuses, or lies; not even the truth. Nothing, you understand? You said, 'Forgive me,' and that's what I've done, and I never want to hear another word about this, all right?" I nodded, swallowing again, and Min stared at me, burst into tears, and said, "Oh, Sam, how *could* you? How could you *do* it? TELL ME! How in the world could you ever do a thing like that!"

So I talked, not in sentences with subjects and predicates that you could diagram on a blackboard, but in murmurs, single words, fragments of phrases, dangling participles, and above all in tones of voice, frequent kisses, and rubbings of the upper and lower back. All this was meant to say—and did say—just one thing, that what had happened really hadn't happened at all. It's what she wanted to hear, it's what

I wanted to tell her, and I murmured, gestured, mumbled, kissed, and stroked this new truth into being. Women, as we all know, are the supreme realists; they understand instinctively how dangerous reality is and the necessity of disguising it, but even in the act of doing so they never lose touch with it. Min put her hands on my forearms, looked straight into my eyes, and said, "Sam, tell me—I want the truth— after I left, did you and Janet . . . ?"

I took her hands, held them tight together between mine, and returned her look squarely and honestly. The passion of truth sounded in my voice as I said, "Min, after you had left me even the notion of anything like that would have been absolutely impossible, and I'd have thought that somehow you'd know that. That's the truth, and may I be struck dead this instant if it isn't." I waited an instant, and another to make sure, then since I still seemed to be alive and I could see that Min believed me, I kissed her and was finally happy.

Later we got up, put on robes, and went out to the kitchen where Min began making coffee as I started mixing drinks. So we did both, and while the coffee was brewing, we wandered out to the patio, drinks in hand. It was nice out, and we stood looking around, feeling good, then we heard the Thunderbird pull into the driveway next door. I walked to the edge of the patio, peeked around the corner of the house, and saw Howie just as he slammed the car door and headed for Janet's, looking pleased. "Wonder where he's been?" I said, casually phrasing the question that had been on my mind for some time.

Min shrugged and said, "How would I know? He was furious with Janet and was just getting dressed to leave when I got here last night. So he dropped me at the Fairmont and went on. I went to bed and slept after a fashion. This morning I got up, took a cable car down California Street to Blum's for breakfast, and saw your message on the billboard directly across the street; so did everyone else on the cable car. I went right back to the hotel, Sam, checked out, and took a cab home."

I smiled, kissed her nose, and said, "What was Howie mad at?"

"Janet simply wouldn't believe he really loved her; she insisted it was her inheritance. They argued all evening. But this time Howie knew better. I guess it was the first time he was absolutely sure of himself. Because they found a brand-new will, Sam, handwritten but perfectly legal, and it doesn't leave Janet a cent. She wasn't home when the lawyer phoned, so he called Howie at the office and told him."

"And that still didn't convince Janet about Howie?"

"No, because naturally Howie didn't tell her she'd lost the inheritance."

"Naturally. But why the hell not?"

"Oh, *Sam*. He didn't want to have to *prove* he loved her; he wanted her to sense that herself."

"I see. How come she doesn't inherit?"

"Her grandfather left all his money to the Communist party."

"*What?*"

"On condition that they divvy it up and disband; he believed in direct action. Howie says it'll drag through the courts for a hundred years."

I took a swallow of my drink and on impulse reached out with my foot, kicked the switch of the mobile, and the thing jumped into action, chugging, clunking, and woofing away. We stood watching it, and the hub caps whirled, glinting splendidly in the morning sun, the tennis racket flailed, the mustached man jiggled up and down, rods rose and fell, wheels spun, and things waggled merrily. "I think I've got the name for that thing," I said to Min. "It just came to me. "

"What is it?"

"Well, look at it, bouncing, jittering, jumping up and down. Busy as all hell, running around in circles, and getting nowhere. And the whole frantic activity completely based on, entirely sustained by, and permanently connected to a bedspring. Only one thing in the world I could possibly call it." I put my arm around Min's waist.

"What's that?"

"Autobiography," I said, and we turned to walk into the house toward the smell of coffee, and Min smiled at me tenderly, then jumped as I reached down and pinched her.